OCEAN

AXE

TARO

BANANAS

BONES
RUM

EGGS

Coconut Island

COCONUT ISLAND

OR

THE ADVENTURES OF TWO CHILDREN
IN THE SOUTH SEAS

Written and Illustrated by

ROBERT GIBBINGS

LETCHWORTH

J. M. DENT & SONS LTD

A 259/3 m

*The first edition of this book
was dedicated to*

PATRICK *and* PENELOPE

*This edition
is dedicated to*

PATRICK'S *daughter* CLEMENCY

and

PENELOPE'S *son* ANTHONY

CONTENTS

CHAPTER ONE

PATRICK, PENELOPE, AND JAMAICA

"OH Misther John, Misther John, what d'ye want with taking them innocent children to be eaten alive by cannibals? Oh Misther John, if their mother knew what you were doin' wid them she'd twist in her grave; the poor woman, and she thinking you'd be taking care of them after she was gone. Oh Miss Penelope, 'tis sad I am to be seein' you going, you with the fine plump figure, you'll never escape; glory be to God, they'll be making steaks of ye before ye're on the island half an hour, and Master Patrick there, with not much but skin on his bones, 'tis

1   A*

tied up he'll be and fattened like a little pig for the market."

"For goodness' sake be quiet, Mary," said Uncle John, "there are no more cannibals in the South Seas than there are in the County Cork."

"Oh wirra wirra! that ye didn't die before ye were born, that I ever reared ye to be making roast joints for them heathens. Leave them behind ye, Mr. John. Go out and draw all the fish in the oceans, but leave them poor little critturs behind you."

"Not so little," said Patrick.

"We're both taller than you," said Penelope.

"Arrah, be quiet and have sinse the two of ye, 'tis small enough ye'll be when ye're in the pot. Yes, Masther Patrick, there'll be no jumping out of that like you used to jump out of the clothes basket to put the fear of heaven into me. Once ye're in the pot 'tis better for ye keep yer head down and simmer gently—or maybe ye'll get a crack on yer skull would hurt ye."

"We're going anyway," said Penelope.

"Of course ye're going, did ye ever stop doin' anything because old Mary told ye not to. Of course ye're going, and if I hadn't the legs bad under me I'd be coming too—just to give the pot a stir."

"Bedtime!" said Uncle John.

Patrick, fair haired and blue eyed, was tall for his thirteen years, and slight. Thanks to an irresponsible father, now dead, his education had been somewhat erratic, but his lack of knowledge from books was amply made up for by his self-reliance and ability to do other things of at least equal importance. He thought nothing of bicycling alone across England or sailing his own dinghy in the open sea in weather that brought the bigger yachts inshore for shelter.

2

Good manners and a sense of humour were likely to see him through. Penelope, a year older, two stone heavier, and her face covered in freckles, was as noisy and untidy as her brother was quiet and orderly. Her laugh could be heard from one end of the hockey field to the other. She was just about where she ought to be in her form, though she could certainly have been higher if she had not been so fond of animals. How could she possibly concentrate on Henry the Second while the groundsmen were doctoring the cricket pitch with chemicals and sweeping up thousands of agonized worms?

But now she was scrubbing her teeth and Patrick was sitting on the side of the bath.

"I'll tell you what," he said, "we'll make a raft and explore the other islands, and we'll make bows and arrows out of bamboo."

"And build a house out of palm trees," spluttered Penelope, "and cook on hot stones," splutter, "breadfruit and paw-paws." Splutter!

"What *are* paw-paws?"

"Don't know, something you eat."

"Uncle John says the natives live on nothing but coconuts and fish."

"That's rot: they must have bananas, and any amount of other fruit, and birds."

"That wouldn't be a desert island."

"But we're not going to a *desert* island."

"Go to *bed*!" roared their uncle.

Uncle John was what old Mary described as "the quietest and the soberest man she'd ever met". He was of middle age and medium build. The few remaining hairs on the top of his head were as fine as the fluff on a chicken, and they shone bright against his sunburnt skull. His face was

3

as brown as a cow, and when he spoke the tip of his nose twitched like a rabbit's. His blue eyes and his crooked mouth seemed always to be holding back a smile. He certainly *was* quiet, and he had the fortunate knack of making himself inconspicuous in any company. Whether he was among the Arabs in Algeria or the Eskimos at Hudson Bay, it was the same thing, no one seemed to notice him. The result was that, being an artist, he had filled countless notebooks with sketches made in strange places and had become one of the leading illustrators of travel books.

Some weeks later all three of them were on board the *St. Lawrence*, a cargo vessel bound for New Zealand via Jamaica and Panama.

"So you're off to the South Seas," said Mr. Pitcher the mate, to Patrick. "And what are you up to down there?"

"Uncle John is illustrating a book, something about tropical fish and coral; he's an artist you know."

"It's being written by a man called MacCarthy who lives in Tahiti," said Penelope. "Ever heard of Uncle?" she asked.

"What's his name?"

"Alexander."

"Don't know much about artists," said Mr. Pitcher, scratching his closely cropped head. "I reckon most of 'em is daft, isn't they?—wears their hair long and goes and paints pictures of carrots, and eggs that look as if they'd been laid all crooked."

"He draws people and animals," said Penelope, "and he *doesn't* wear his hair long."

"Hasn't got enough of it!" said Patrick.

The first three days had been raw and cold, with patches of fog, but by the fourth morning the sun was shining and

4

everyone felt more cheerful. In the afternoon the first flying fish were seen, breaking from the ship's bow. These creatures, no bigger than herrings, flipped over the wave crests to fall in the sea some fifty yards away. By next morning they were shooting from the water in shoals, as many as fifteen, twenty or even thirty together.

"They're good for eating, they are," said "Slushy", the cook. "Sometimes they fly on board at night and we fry 'em."

"Are *all* fish eatable?" asked Penelope.

"Well, I reckon most of 'em is, leastways them near home; but there's the Muki-Muki at Honolulu, if you eat him you're a gonner, and they say as how them Globe fishes is poisonous—but who wants to eat a pin cushion? Not me, anyway!"

On the thirteenth day out, the *St. Lawrence* reached Jamaica. The children were on deck early, and from a distance they could see along the coast a fringe of palm trees with, here and there, clearings covered with bushy cocoa or coffee shrubs.

As they drew closer a warm tropic smell was wafted to them from the land, and when they came on deck after breakfast the ship was already in harbour and officials were coming on board from small launches.

A fleet of "bum boats" had begun to trade with the crew. These ramshackle craft were loaded down with fruit, dried coral, conch shells, native-made chairs and hats.

The owner of one of the boats had thrown a rope to a sailor; halfway down was a basket of oranges.

"How much?" called the sailor, hauling it on board.

"One sheeling, saar, one sheeling, very naice fruit, saar."

"Give you tuppence," called the sailor.

"No, saar, they varee fresh fruit, I give them you ten-pence, varee cheap, varee fresh."

"I'll give you thrippence."

"You give me eightpence, saar, you keep them."

"Thrippence or nothing."

"Oh, saar, dat no good to me, I pay seexpence only jest one hour back."

"Thrippence," said the sailor.

"Oh, saar, you give me fourpence, I lose money but I give dem to you."

"Fourpence?"

"Yes, saar! I take it."

"Done!" called the sailor, and putting the money into the basket he lowered away.

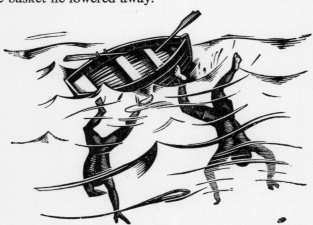

While they were watching further bargains being made, two small boys, wearing diminutive pants, appeared in a rickety boat.

7

"Throw seexpence, lady! Throw seexpence, seexpence in water, lady, we dive."

"Try them with a penny," said Uncle John.

As the coin struck the water one of the boys plunged overboard, and appeared a moment later with it in his teeth. Then Uncle John tried them with two pennies, whereupon they nearly upset their cockleshell; but they were soon back, one with a copper in his mouth, the other holding it between his toes.

At this moment Mr. Pitcher came along to say that all was clear for landing, and the doctor would take them ashore. No need of a second hint; they were soon bobbing up and down in the launch.

"Phew, it's hot," said Penelope, as they stepped ashore.

"Bit of a stink, too," said Patrick.

They hadn't walked a dozen yards before they were accosted by a negro chauffeur.

"Dis way to de town, saar, you like motor car, saar, me very good driver, fine car, saar, my car best car in town, saar, my name Ebeneezer, me best driver in town, saar, I'll take you see—"

"No," said Alexander, "we're going to walk."

"Too hot walk, saar, much better drive wid me, two pounds de whole day you go where you like, I wait for you where you like."

"You wait where you are," said Alexander, "we're going to walk."

"Penny please," said a small voice behind Penelope. She looked round to see a tiny black urchin clad in a pink shirt and an enormous hat.

"Penny please," he repeated, "me no fadder, no mudder, poor sad boy, penny please."

She was about to give him something when her uncle

8

intervened. "For heaven's sake," he said, "don't give any-one anything, or we'll have the whole island following us."

So they wandered about till they found a café where they could sit in the open and watch the passers-by.

"How would you like to carry that?" said Uncle John, as a native woman strolled by, balancing a basket of melons on her head.

"Look at that poor unfortunate little donkey," said Penelope, "with baskets on either side and that huge black woman on top, and there's a child with a whole crate of oranges on its head."

All the men were dressed in white, and with their black faces and hands they looked like a photographic negative of people in England whose clothes are so black and whose faces and hands are so white.

In the market place they found pots and pans of red clay, baskets of pineapples, custard apples, and avocado pears; ranged on the ground were sweet potatoes, yams and all kinds of strange roots. There were piles of beans and pyramids of breadfruit. "That's what caused the mutiny in the *Bounty*," said Uncle John.

"I know," said Patrick. "Captain Bligh and Tahiti, they were bringing breadfruit here and the crew mutinied and they went off to some island or other."

"Pitcairn," said Alexander.

"And they threw all the trees overboard and they all murdered each other and a British ship went out and brought them back prisoners and some were hung, but some were let off."

"Penny please," said a small voice behind Penelope. "Penny please, me no fadder, no mudder, me pore sad boy."

But before there was time to answer, the youthful beggar had been pushed aside by their would-be chauffeur.

"You want motor car, saar, me very good driver, saar, I show you all de things to see, saar, all de tombs of de kings and de admirals and de generals; all very sad, very mournful, very amusin'."

"Penny please?"

"You run away home to yore mudder, you little black nuisance. What will yore fadder say if he catch you discompose white gen'leman? Don't you take no notice, saar. You run along home now, you little black chocolate box."

"Where can we get lunch?" asked Alexander.

"Oh saar, de Myrtle Bank, dat is quite de best, very good food, saar, and I wait for you and take you Port Antonio or de Castleton Gardens or show you de fort of Lord Nelson or de Gallows Point where de pirates was hung."

"Too expensive: we want somewhere cheap."

"Oh saar, you come wid me, saar, I take you visit my cousin, she cook most tastefully and she have very beautiful garden, saar, my cousin got all de fruit in de world in her garden, saar, guavas, mangoes, custard apples. Oh yes, saar, she grows melons and pomegranates and de golden apples. There is not any kind of fruit in heaven that my cousin does not grow."

"What do you know about heaven?" asked Alexander.

"Wal, I know more than some of dem preachers, saar, leastways I think dey all wrong say we made of dust. Why saar, dust all fall into little pieces; p'raps we made of cement that stick together—make mighty good bones."

His car was standing a few yards away. Uncle John got into it in front beside their guide and the children scrambled in behind.

"Where are you taking us, anyway?"

"Why, saar, I take you jest along to my cousin near by de Castleton Gardens only very few miles from de town, saar. She have de most beautiful fruit in Jamaica, and den I take you see de Gardens and den back to de ship.

"Dat tree wid de yellow nuts is de real genuine cocoa tree, missy; sometimes de nuts is purple, but all de same thing, when they's ripe, they's heaped together and slashed open wid de big knive and de women they dance on them and de cocoa beans fall out all round and polished."

"That might take *your* weight down," said Patrick, to Penelope.

"Shut up! Are all those trees bananas?" she asked the driver.

"Oh yes, missy, there's plenty banana trees in dis island, but each tree only grow one bunch, then we cut him down and he start all over again."

"For heaven's sake look where you're driving," said Alexander, as they barely escaped another car coming round the corner.

"Yes, saar, they very careless drivers these coloured gen'lemen, they never do seem to know which left of de road is de right."

Then they drove through a wooded valley with tall tree ferns on either side. Water trickled down the slopes and crossed the road in shallow streams through which the car bumped and splashed. Green and crimson parrots screeched loudly overhead, and flocks of doves fluttered among the trees.

"Where's that cousin of yours?" said Alexander.

"Why, saar, we just arrivin' at this very precise moment." Pulling up the car with a jerk, Ebeneezer honk-honked with his horn till his cousin and her husband and her five black children all came rushing out to see what the noise was about.

11

" 'Allo, 'Epsibah, dese friends of mine want Jamaica dinner and very good supply of fruit."

"Why, yes, saar, my cousin Ebeneezer, he bring you to de very most right place, you come with me, saar—dis way, saar. Now mind de step and take great care of yore head under dese trees."

She led them to a verandah shaded by masses of deep bougainvillea, that marvellous flowering climber which the French explorer Bougainville seems to have left all over the tropics. On the slope below them grew tobacco plants, while on the other side of the valley the branches of the trees glistened with ripe oranges sparkling in the sun.

They were hardly seated when Hepsibah seized a broom, jumped from the balcony and dashed behind the house. In a few moments she came back, panting: "Oh, saar, please 'scuse me, saar, dat dam' mongoose again, he kill my chickens."

She wiped her shiny face. "Yes, saar, dese mongooses am most important nuisance. Some fellow once bring dem in dis island for to kill de rats and de snakes but now dey kill all de chickens and de birds—why, saar, dere is no birds left to eat de ticks on de cattle, my father say he much rather have de rats. Now, saar, I fry you some flying fish; my daughter Carmel, she jest bring dem fresh from market, and then, saar, I give you very tender little pigs' trotters with baked bananas."

"I'm dying of thirst," said Patrick.

"One moment, saar, I make you fine lemon squash double quick. Yes, missy, I make for you too. Carmel,

12

Car—mel," she shouted. "Go pick lemons for make squash."

Then the children could hear the sounds of cooking and they had not long to wait before the flying fish appeared on the table.

After that came the promised trotters and bananas and then more fruit than they could eat in a week. Eventually they could hardly move, but they were too near the famous Castleton Gardens to miss seeing them.

Here was every imaginable kind of tree and flowering shrub: the fan-shaped traveller's palm, so called because there is always water at its base; the strelitzia with its blooms like lobsters' claws, and all kinds of venomous-looking cacti. Brightly coloured humming birds and little green tody birds, with their crimson breasts, hovered amongst the flowers, and the black and yellow honey-suckers hopped from branch to branch, peeping into the blossoms and picking out the insects they found within.

But Ebeneezer was waiting to drive them back to the ship, and there was no time to explore the island, not even time to visit Fort Charles where Nelson, as a young officer, had once been in command. "Dey call de ramparts alongside of his house de quarter-deck of Lord Nelson," said Ebeneezer.

An hour later the children and their uncle were steaming out of harbour and heading south for the Panama Canal.

That evening the Captain told them of the famous "Shark Papers" that are still to be seen in the Jamaica Museum. "There was a brig called the *Nancy*," he said. "It would be back in about the year 1800, and she was up to some sort of piracy or smuggling. A British ship captured her and, thinking there was something fishy about her, so to speak, the Captain sent her papers ashore to be examined by the authorities. There *was* something fishy sure enough, for while the case was being examined, everything seemed to be in order, but just at the last moment, when the brig was about to be released, a young naval officer came in with a bundle of ship's papers which he had found in the stomach of a shark he'd caught. These papers turned out to be the real papers of the *Nancy*. The others were fakes. You see, when the captain of the *Nancy* saw that he was going to be captured, he threw overboard all the papers that proved he was a pirate. But a shark will always go for anything that makes a splash in the water, and one just came along and swallowed the whole bundle of papers, and as luck would have it, soon after that, it swallowed a chunk of meat that had a hook in it."

"What happened to the pirates?" asked Patrick.

"I don't know what happened to the pirates," said the Captain, "but the head of the shark is now in the United Services Museum in London and anyone can go and see it."

The next day was their last on the *St. Lawrence*, as they were due at Colon the following morning.

"You take care of yourselves if you get to Papua," said Mr. Pitcher, "there's a village there called 'the place for roasting the guests'."

"And don't go tattooing your faces," said Sparks, the wireless officer.

"Of course we wouldn't," said Penelope.

"Of course you would," ragged Sparks, "if it was the fashion. Doesn't your sister paint her lips and pluck her eyebrows? And don't you pierce your nose with a bone ring," he added. "Remember white girls only pierce their ears for gold rings."

14

Alexander had reckoned that they might have to wait a week or more before catching the French mail boat to Tahiti, but, as it turned out, the first thing they saw in harbour was a ship called the *Hineanna* taking in ballast. It appeared that a cousin of Mr. Pitcher's was on board and that she was bound for the Society Islands to bring back phosphate.

"Any room for passengers?" signalled Pitcher.

"Three small ones," replied his cousin.

"Send a boat," said Pitcher.

Here was luck—sailing that very morning, no hanging about in a stuffy town, no trouble with customs. All they had to do was follow their baggage into the waiting boat. Hurried goodbyes, and ten minutes later they were on board their new ship.

"It's rough fare," said the Captain, "and cramped quarters. We drop a few stores at Cocos and after that no more land for eighteen days."

"Cocos?" asked Patrick excitedly. "You mean the Cocos Islands where all the treasure is buried?"

"Yes, and treasure hunters too! There's a party down there now."

"Have they found anything?"

"Not much, I guess. One of 'em's a water diviner, says he can find gold with his rod. Says he can tell if you have a sovereign in your pocket. I reckon there's more than a pair of pants down there between him and the gold."

Soon the *Hineanna* began to move towards the great locks which were to raise her ninety feet on the first stage of her journey through the canal. Hawsers were passed ashore and the ship was slowly drawn into the first of the three great water chambers. Quietly and steadily the steel

15

gates closed behind them and the water rose, inch by inch, foot by foot, until they were floating thirty feet or more above their previous level. Then without any noise, without even a word of command being heard, the gates ahead opened, and they moved into the second lock. From there into the third great reservoir and so on to the Gatun lake.

After about eight hours' steaming, watching the rich tropical vegetation on either side of the lake, and seeing

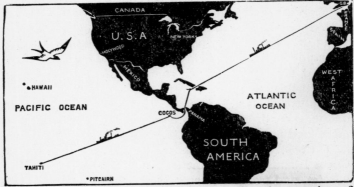

the dead tops of the submerged trees like the remains of some primeval forest, they reached the western end of the canal where another series of locks brought them down to the level of the Pacific. The canal hands then went ashore, and the children saw the bow of their ship heading for the open sea.

It was good to be away from the muggy atmosphere of the canal zone and to see the whole Pacific stretching before them. Four thousand miles to the north-west lay the Hawaiian islands and Honolulu, four thousand miles to the south-west lay Tahiti and the Tuamotu Archipelago. What ho, for the South Seas!

16

On the second day out they sighted the Cocos Islands. Then, as they came near, a launch was seen coming to meet them to collect stores.

"Found anything?" shouted Patrick, while boxes were being lowered over the side.

"Bones," was the reply.

"Seen anything of pirates?"

"Bones," was the reply.

The launch pushed off, the ship gathered speed, and soon the white sand and the palm-fringed shore were low on the horizon.

"The treasure's there all right," said the Captain, "plenty of it, but there's been a landslide and no one will ever find it. I don't believe much in clues myself. If I buried a lot of money I wouldn't go putting up signposts to tell everyone where it was. No! The secret went with old Keating. He brought away twenty thousand pounds, but he died before he could get any more."

"Is there much left, do you think?"

"Millions! Millions! All these blooming pirates found it a safe spot for their loot, and few of them ever got back for it. But the whole island is wild jungle and mountains and it's six miles across, so there's plenty to dig. After all, a few sacks of gold don't take much hiding."

Patrick went to bed with the firm intention of going there one day to try his luck. He felt that if only he could invent a compass which would point towards gold instead of towards steel all would be well.

After that it was eighteen lazy days with never a sight of ship or land, only the flying fish breaking from the bows and an occasional whale spouting in the distance.

"There's no doubt this ship was mentioned in the

Bible," murmured Mr. Pitcher's cousin, "when it says God created all creeping things."

"You go back to your mail boat," retorted the second engineer.

"Not me. Three clean collars every day?—one blinking muffler per trip does me."

"What time do we arrive?" asked Penelope.

"Five o'clock tomorrow afternoon you'll be ashore."

CHAPTER TWO

TAHITI

TAHITI at last. For two hours or more the cloud-capped hills had been drawing nearer; from a faint line on the horizon they grew into jagged spires emerging from heavily wooded slopes. Then a line of white breakers betrayed the encircling reef, and soon the small town of Papeete showed itself sitting on the edge of the lagoon.

At a given moment the bows of the *Hineanna* swung towards the shore and the ship moved from the deep blue of the ocean, through the break in the reef, into the clear lagoon.

Their rooms at the Hotel Tahiti opened on to a wide

verandah overlooking the harbour. For meals other than breakfast they would have to go to the Tiare Hotel or one of the numerous Chinese cafés.

But they didn't want food just then; they wanted to see the town.

They were surprised to find that all the natives were dressed like Europeans, that there were no naked savages running about with clubs and spears, and that the wooden houses were very much the same as they had seen in Jamaica. When they turned into the side streets they saw that most of the shops were owned by Chinese. At the door of each emporium the proprietor was standing, all smiles, ready to sell them anything from a grand piano to a collar stud. They read over the doors such names as YAT LEE, AI YU, and MOO FAT. They thought Moo Fat's name very appropriate. He was extremely stout.

Children abounded everywhere, half-caste Chinese with their little brown heads close shaven. Native girls passed by in smart cotton frocks, native men rode about on bicycles. A frightful din was heard as a motor truck approached with youths banging kerosene tins to attract attention to the cinema posters that they carried. There was a shop window filled with sharks' jaws, carved coconuts and shell necklaces. There was a wooden church and a tin garage.

Turning to the right, they reached the water-front again to find a party of girls bathing. These did not bother about the latest style in bathing dresses; they just went into the water in their everyday clothes, and afterwards went home and changed into a dry outfit.

But the sun was already low on the horizon and a cool breeze was coming down from the mountains. They found their way to the "Tiare" and were shown to a table on the spacious verandah overlooking the garden.

A girl brought garlands of flowers to hang round their necks. A party of natives with guitars was sitting on the lawn singing; myna birds, like brightly coloured starlings, chattered in the trees; two green lizards chased each other along the railing. Other clients, some white, some coloured, began to drop in and soon there was hardly a spare seat. It was one of the nights given up to "native food", and that always brought a crowd.

The talk was partly in English, partly in French. Before they had got very far with their meal someone suggested that all the tables should be joined into one big one so as to make the party more friendly. This done, the little red-faced man on their left introduced himself as Tomlinson. "But you call me Tommy," he said; "everyone calls me Tommy, by golly, they do. I'm down here on holiday, this is my wife Hina. You've only just arrived? Well, half a mo' and you'll know everyone. That good-looking fellow opposite is Brooke, Clymer Brooke; he came from America in a yacht and liked the place so much he built a house and stayed here. Those two at the end of the table with the pretty girl between them are Hall and his wife and Nord-hoff—clever blokes, by golly, they are, written a lot of books about the *Bounty*, famous they are, famous all over the world—we're mighty proud of them we are, good fellows, oh, by gum, they're good fellows all right. Now that big handsome dark chap halfway down the table is Bill Bambridge, he belongs to the island, a fine dancer. He helped Flaherty with his South Sea films, acted in them too, he did—and wait till you hear him with the concertina, he'd sing the heart out of your mouth.

"Here's the fish, nothing like native cooking, best in the

21

world. Bring us some more limes, Emma! There, isn't that good? These fish never been near a fire, cooked in lime juice only. You see that fellow just behind the pillar, that's Stimson, he's a scientist, written books about the native life; and that's Jones just beyond him, fine brains too. Yes, we've lots of brains in Tahiti, I'm the only one without them. I haven't any at all, look at my head, too small, no room for them. I'm a trader. What are you?"

"I'm an artist," said Alexander.

"Thought you were," said Tommy, "you've got the look in your eye."

"Do you know a man called MacCarthy, a scientist?"

"You mean Larry Mac, the fish man; by golly, I do—no chin, pointed nose, just like a fish himself. He loves 'em, been up with me at Marutea, studying colour changes he was, says all the fish we thought was different are the same, it's only their age is different. I'd never have believed it, I swear I wouldn't, by golly no!"

The sucking pig now arrived, served with breadfruit and sweet potatoes. It was so tender that it seemed more like chicken than pork, and the breadfruit tasted like a mixture of potatoes and bananas. The sweet potatoes had a pleasant flavour of chestnuts.

"Go slow, or you'll have a roaring pain tonight," said Uncle John.

" No pain, no pain, *pas du tout*," said Hina; "plenty *uru* in tummy, no pain."

"Quite right," said Tommy; "eat plenty *uru*, that's breadfruit, and you can digest tin-tacks."

The girls had brought in their guitars from the garden and everyone was calling on Atu-tahi for a dance.

When he took the floor, the band played louder and faster. Everyone began to sing and to stamp their feet in

22

time with the music, and one after another the girls stood up and danced with him. Facing each other, laughing and clapping their hands, they danced with swift and swinging rhythm; their feet moved little, but their bodies turned and twisted, their hips swinging faster and faster as the tempo of the music increased, till at last they dropped exhausted into their chairs.

It was nearly midnight when the party broke up.

Tommy accompanied them to the hotel. "See you in the morning," he said. "I'll help you to find MacCarthy."

Penelope couldn't sleep, no matter how she twisted and turned, no matter how she banged her pillow. She could hear the surf booming on the reef, she could hear mosquitoes trying to get inside her net, she could hear her uncle's snores: but whenever she composed herself for sleep she seemed to feel the motion of the ship she had just left, and she started up, fearing that after all she had not yet arrived and that the events of the day had been all a dream.

Just when the first glint of dawn was showing in the sky she heard footsteps in the street below. She listened: not one but several people were passing—she could hear voices chattering. The whole town seemed to be awake.

She got up and, peeping over the verandah, saw everyone walking in the same direction and carrying baskets. Hastily dressing, she slipped downstairs and mingled with the passers-by. Following the crowd, she found herself in the market place, where everyone on the island seemed to have gathered.

The fruit was much the same as in Jamaica, except that it was tied up in queer baskets. Some were shallow with long handles, some were deep with no handles, some were wide open, others were woven entirely round their contents; most of them were made of coconut fronds, but the oranges were strung together in nets of fibre.

In amongst the fruit and the vegetables, the squeaking pigs and the brightly coloured fish, were native-made hats, rolls of palm matting, bales of cotton, and joints of raw meat. Everywhere people were driving bargains.

Penelope suddenly became aware that it was broad daylight and that she was ravenously hungry. Retracing her steps, she soon found a street leading to the sea, and from there it was no trouble to find her way back to the hotel.

Uncle John was waiting for her on the verandah. He was not in the least alarmed at her absence, for news travels quickly in Tahiti and he had already been told about her doings.

Patrick appeared while they were talking, and they settled down to breakfast. Below them the lagoon reflected the cloudless sky; a schooner tied to the wharf shone dazzling white; an outrigger canoe lay on the grass in the shadow of the scarlet-blossomed flamboyant trees.

"First thing," said Uncle John, "is to find MacCarthy." So, having finished their coffee, they set out for the Post Office, on chance of a letter.

No, there was nothing for them.

But yes!—the postmaster knew Monsieur MacCarthy. He lived at the twenty kilometre mark from town; he hadn't been in for his last mails. They thought he'd gone to one of the low islands. It would be better to ask at the Consul's.

The Consul could give no information. If MacCarthy was expecting them, and they hadn't heard from him, he was bound to turn up in a week or two. Had they enquired at Donald's store? There might be a message through the firm's shipping agents.

24

On the way to Donald's they had to pass their hotel, and there in the café was Tommy waiting for them.

"Found Mac?" he asked.

"No," said Alexander.

"Nor have I. Not a sign, not a blinking sign. Ellis at the garage thinks he's at Papeari on the other side of the island, but Delmain, the harbour master, says he's gone on a schooner. Wait a moment, there's Amundsen. Say, captain, come to our table, meet Mr. Alexander and family."

The big blond Dane sat down.

"They've just arrived from England," said Tommy, "and they want to find Larry Mac, the fish man."

"I know whar he ees, und I am the onlee white perrson in the worrld who knows whar he ees."

"Where's that?" said Tommy.

"Motu Marama," said Amundsen.

"Where's that?" asked Alexander.

"In thee low isle-lands thirty miles sout of Makemo. My sheep left him thar."

"Are you going back soon?"

"Yas! I go next week. I go Monday or I go Tuesday, perhaps I go Wednesday, if you want passage you must see Smeeth. When my sheep ready we go fetch copra from Makemo and Marutea and Nihiru, but you must see Smeeth. Yas, I take you Marama, but you go see Smeeth. P'raps we sail Monday if wind blow good."

So off they went to see Mr. Smith, the owner of the schooner *Rupe*. "Tahitian for 'dove', " said Tommy, "and Motu Marama means 'island of the moon'. When you get there you'll find the lagoon like a big crescent with all the little islands dotted round the edge."

"Are there savages?" asked Penelope.

"Savages, no, but natives, lots of 'em: they'll fix you up

with a house, Larry Mac will see to that. Fine chap, Larry."

They found Mr. Smith in his office. He was quite agreeable to give them a passage, provided they shared the only cabin. "Don't know when she sails, engine being overhauled; perhaps O.K. Monday, p'raps Tuesday. I'll let you know."

So they had four days in which to amuse themselves.

The children didn't mind the delay. There was plenty to see and do, even if it was only to mooch about the waterfront and watch the schooners coming and going, being loaded and unloaded. On one of the schooners which was going to the Marquesas Islands they saw bags of flour, cases of beef, and tins of biscuits being put on board. In addition, there were rolls of rope, drums of kerosene, and sheets of roofing iron. These were supplies for the trading stores, and the schooner would return to Tahiti with a cargo of dried coconut (which is known as copra), coffee-beans and oranges. Another schooner had just arrived from the Tuamotus with pearl shell. They watched sack after sack of it being brought ashore—about fifty ton, they were told. It is not for pearls that the natives dive, up in the Tuamotus, but for the shell that is so valuable for making pearl buttons, knife handles, and many other things. The chance of finding a pearl inside a shell is very small, perhaps only one in every thousand.

Another schooner, a big three-master, had brought in a load of phosphate from Makatea. On that island, as on Ocean Island, sea birds have nested for thousands and thousands of years, and because there is no rain to wash away the droppings of the birds, these have accumulated and dried into a hard rock which, when broken up, makes the splendid fertiliser that we know as guano. There was a schooner, too, that had carried no cargo when she came into harbour. Three months earlier, during a storm, she had been thrown on a reef and had lain there for eight weeks, buffeted by the waves, until, after being emptied of all her cargo, a high sea had carried her back into deep water. Now she was waiting to go into dock and have her timbers repaired.

Tommy pointed out to them a strange-looking craft, on which he said he had once made a voyage. "Twenty-two days it took us," he said, "instead of four as we'd expected. No engine, and sails made of bed sheeting—she can't sail to windward. Her captain doesn't hold with spending money on old ships. He won't even buy an anchor—uses a lump of coral or a bit of an old motor car. He says, 'An anchor's a valuable thing—can't afford to lose that.' Yes, I travelled in her—three foot of headroom for the passengers, on top of a load of dry fish; cockroaches by the thousand, and the water in the iron drums so rusty it looked like coffee.

"You must get mats," continued Tommy, "palm mats, one each, and a pillow, that's all you want. Then you can sleep anywhere; no one carries more in the Islands."

On Monday they were told that the repairs would be finished by Tuesday, and on Tuesday they were told they could not be completed till Wednesday, and on Wednesday it was cinema night in town and the crew wouldn't sail.

On Thursday the *Rupe* was ready—then at last they found themselves on board, with the engine chug-chugging and the schooner heading for the open sea. Once through the reef, the sails were hoisted and the vessel heeled over in the breeze.

Captain Amundsen was in great form. At sea he could get rid of his collar and shoes, and now he stood barefooted,

27

in trousers and vest, leaning against the deck house, with arms crossed, smacking his huge biceps, and laughing as the warm spray splashed over and hit him on the chest.

"Goot wind, goot wind, queek treep, queek treep."

As they drew away from the land the wind freshened and they bowled along, sailing due east for the island of Anaa. With weather like this they would reach Marama in three days.

But by Saturday the wind was heading them, and they were compelled to steer a more northerly course. That same evening it dropped altogether and they lay becalmed with sails flapping. The sea became oily smooth, a shark came and looked up at them and went away again. The *Rupe* rolled horribly. Penelope felt sick and Patrick was sick. Uncle John looked green and drank whisky. All night the rigging creaked; they wondered why they had ever left Tahiti. Who wanted to see a beastly coral island anyway?

28

No, they didn't want any filthy tea out of a tin can, all they wanted was to be left alone. Eventually they dropped off to sleep and dreamt of London and hard pavements that didn't rock under their feet.

Next morning a breeze came in from the northwest, the sails filled, and with the wind behind them they regained all the ground they had lost on the previous day.

They sighted gulls ahead. "Fish! Bonito!" exclaimed Amundsen. "Whar dem rods?" he shouted excitedly.

One of the crew handed him a bamboo pole about ten feet long. It had a cord of its own length and the hook was a wedge of pearl shell with a point cut from turtle shell lashed at one end. A few pig's bristles helped to disguise the point and resembled a fish's tail when dragged through the water.

As the *Rupe* bore down on the screaming gulls Amundsen cast the hook into the water. It had hardly touched the surface when Patrick was felled to the deck by a huge fish which caught him full in the chest. He got up, furious, just in time to see first one and then another drop in Penelope's lap. She screamed and scrambled to her feet, but as she did so another caught her midways; she bumped into Patrick, and both, losing their balance, rolled on the deck amongst the flapping bonitos.

By this time they were through the shoal, and Amundsen looked round to see his catch.

"Wat game you playing wid my feesh?" he asked. "You

29

must note stand in the way, thar ees no barrrb on the hook, I jump them off queek, queek."

The *Rupe* rushed on, always just ahead of the white-capped waves which chased her.

But towards the afternoon the sky had begun to thicken and the glass was falling. Amundsen had lost his cheerfulness; he said little and watched the sky.

"Storrm, storrm," he muttered.

"I think when I land you Marama I leaf you queek, I think p'raps I geef you thee boat—yes, I geef you thee boat and you land at thee sout' pass, then you rhow along lagoon and you find yore friend on thee nord islet. One day soon I come back fetch the boat. I must take the sheep to sea. If the storm catch us, we fineesh on reef."

The wind was coming in from the south and steadily increasing, the glass was falling lower and lower, the sea was leaden and the dark palms on Marama showed light against the heavy sky.

"I think you best on thee island, I think you note like storrm at sea. Eef wind blow hard, you stay safe where you land till all fineesh, then you go along find your friend next day."

It was almost dusk before they were close enough to launch the boat.

"Eef you keep dose two trees straight in one line you arre pairfectly safe, it ees a wide pass, and if you wait for thee wave it will take you in."

Uncle John took the oars and pulled towards the reef. The children sat in the stern.

"Wait for a beeg wave," shouted Amundsen as the schooner stood out to sea.

The swell was breaking all along the edge of the reef and

great waves were surging through the pass. As each one spent its force the water gushed back to be caught by the next invading swell. It was certainly not a pleasant prospect. The wind was coming in squalls and there were occasional spurts of rain.

The two palm trees were in line, but it was almost impossible to control the boat; currents pulled her this way and that, and gusts of wind, catching her bow, blew her out of line.

Amundsen had said "wait for the wave", but it was too late now, for the boat was being rushed into the rapids, and Alexander could not row fast enough to control it.

Now she was broadside on and being hurled against the coral—no, she was through the gap.

A moment's pause. Could he hold her?

The receding current caught the boat and carried it seawards as though it had been a cork. Then, in the very centre of the pass, they met the next wave.

A moment's horror—over and over and over—swim—must swim—over and over again, can't swim—air—drowning! Air! Air! They were ready to explode before they reached the surface.

Before Penelope had time to look around another wave had swept over her. This time she was carried far up the strand and her frock, catching in some dead coral, held her high and dry.

Patrick fared somewhat better, for being lighter in weight, the first wave had carried him ashore and he was now sitting above high-water line, rubbing his eyes, completely dazed by a bump on the head.

But there was no sign of the boat or of Uncle John.

CHAPTER THREE

MAROONED

A LOUD hiccup from Penelope drew Patrick's attention. This was about the only occasion in his life when
that particular form of noise failed to make him laugh. He
blinked at her across the white sand and again she hiccupped
violently.

He rubbed his eyes.

"Where's Uncle?" he asked.

"Don't know."

"Where's the boat?"

"Don't know."

"We'd better try to find them."

They staggered to their feet. Penelope lurched to one
side, produced some thunderous gurgitations, and was
sick. Having got rid of the salt water she felt better, but
Patrick was still dizzy.

It was growing dark as they wandered along the shore,
searching for any sign of their uncle. On their left was a
line of scrub and small bushes through which the tall stems
of the palms stretched away up to a dark canopy of fronds.
On their right, the lagoon was outlined by the white surf
on the reef against the black sea beyond. They knew that
their uncle was a good swimmer, and anyway the boat
would have floated even if it was upside down. Perhaps he
had been carried in the other direction?

They retraced their steps, but by the time they reached
the scene of their landing it was too dark to go farther.

"Better find somewhere to sleep," said Penelope.

"Better stay where we are," said Patrick. "We don't know what's behind that scrub."

"My clothes are soaking."

"So are mine."

Stripping to their pants, they sat miserably in the sand hugging their knees. How were they going to get through the night? Was it safe to go to sleep? They huddled closer to each other, staring into the darkness.

"This *is* a bit of a do," said Penelope. "I think old Mary was right after all—wish I'd never come."

"Go on!" said Patrick, "when Uncle turns up in the morning you'll feel different."

"S'pose he doesn't turn up, s'pose he's drowned, s'pose we never get off this island?"

Heavy squalls of wind were blowing in from the sea and the surf boomed louder on the reef.

"Captain Amundsen will come back for us, anyway."

"In a week's time, when we're dead."

"Let's go to sleep."

"Good night."

But lying there, with her eyes wide open, Penelope's mind went over and over the things that had just happened, and over and over all the things that might be going to happen. She wondered if there were snakes or other wild creatures in the long grass behind them. Would she be awakened by some animal's warm breath in her face? What had happened to her uncle? Patrick had suggested that he might have been picked up by the natives, but that didn't seem likely. It was a comforting thought, anyway, that Captain Amundsen would come back. She wriggled a hole for her hip in the sand.

"Wasn't it awful when we upset?" she said. "Did you think you were drowned?"

"Didn't think anything . . . I was hit on the head."

"I thought I'd bust, couldn't move in that current, swallowed gallons."

"Let's go to sleep."

"Good night," said Penelope, "I can't think where the boat is," she added. "And the oars, they ought to be floating about."

"DO let's go to sleep," said Patrick.

"'Spect uncle will be along in the morning."

"Um—m . . ."

Just when the world had all the appearance of the inside of a pearl shell, when sky and sea were merged in a shimmering glory of light radiating through every shade of rose, aquamarine and emerald, just at that moment Patrick was awakened by cold water at his feet. Penelope, too, sat up to find the water not only lapping round her toes, but creeping steadily up her legs.

This was all the more surprising as they had taken care to lie down well above the tide mark; and though there is rarely more than eighteen inches rise and fall of tide in these latitudes, the water had already risen several feet and was now covering the grass behind the sand.

There were no waves, there was no wind, the surface of the sea was like undulating glass, and it crept higher and higher.

It was even flowing into the low land behind the protecting beach. The whole foreshore was covered, and the children, ankle deep in water, were aghast.

"What's happening now," said Penelope; "a high tide?"

"A blooming flood," said Patrick.

"What are we going to do?"

"Drown, I should think."

"Might as well have done that yesterday."

Between where they were standing and the nearest land there was now thirty yards of lake, and the water was quickly creeping up their legs.

"There doesn't seem to be anyone on the island," said Penelope. "How low it is!"

"There's a bit of a hill over there," said Patrick, pointing to the left.

"Come on, let's get there quick."

Without waiting any longer, they splashed their way through the undergrowth towards the only high land that was visible. Every now and again they tripped, or they fell and had to swim; they stubbed their toes on unseen objects, they cut their limbs on thorns. But eventually the ground began to rise and each step brought them into shallower water. Soon they were on high land, a dozen feet or more above the flood.

All around them the half-submerged palms were reflected in the water, the undergrowth was completely covered, the only land they could see was the small patch on which they were standing; and all the time the water was rising, slowly and steadily.

Now they were really horrified, as they looked about and saw themselves alone on a few square yards of dry land with, apparently, the whole of the rest of the world under water. In comparison, old man Noah had a comfortable time, for he, at any rate, had his family and the animals to keep him company and, if the rain did go on, the ark would continue to float. But these two children were utterly alone with this devastating sea creeping up and over everything. Was it the end of the world? It seemed like it for them, anyway. Where were their uncle and the boat? They could only suppose he had been drowned. One thing was certain, there was no one else on the island. Everywhere they looked there was only water, and the trees protruding from it.

The water was now lapping at their feet. If only they had had a bit of rope and if only the trees had sloped, they might have been able to climb one of them in the way they had seen the natives do in Tahiti, but the three palms which stood on this one piece of dry land were all as straight and smooth as telegraph poles.

"We can swim to those low ones over there," said Patrick.

"And when they're covered we can swim back to the tops of these," said Penelope.

"And when they're covered?"

"Come on, don't let's talk about it."

The two of them struck out for the palm whose fronds were waving only a few feet above the water. Pulling themselves up by the trailing fronds, they climbed into the heart of the tree.

37

"Plenty of nuts," said Penelope.

"Strikes me we're done," said Patrick.

It certainly did seem that they had little chance as they squatted there among the branches, watching the water creep higher and higher. When the morning haze dispersed they could see other small islands dotted about on the horizon.

"Miles away," said Patrick.

"Five," said Penelope.

"Ten," said Patrick.

They wondered if by any chance their uncle had reached one of them. They wished they were there—it might have been better, it couldn't be worse. They were feeling about as miserable as any two people could be, stuck in the top of a bally old coconut tree without their clothes, plonk in the middle of the Pacific and with the whole blooming ocean spread around them—just about sixty million miles of it.

Of course they ought never to have survived; they ought never to have got back to the boarding schools in England where they are now, continually getting into trouble for talking in class. But if they had been drowned this book would never have been written, for there would have been no one to tell the tale.

The fact is that while they were arguing as to how far away the other islands might be, the sea had begun to go down. Patrick was the first to notice it when he found that his foot was no longer in the water.

"It's going down," he said.

"It's what?"

"Going down, I said. Going down! My foot's out of water."

"It is!" shrieked Penelope. "It is! I can see the mark on

the trees." She began to jump about in wild excitement, and
then it was she herself who went down with a mighty splash
into the water, accompanied by a couple of coconuts on
which she had put her weight.

Her head and the nuts bobbed to the surface at the same
time. "Save the nuts," shouted Patrick, as she clambered
back on to her perch.

Then with the waters abating and the new hope of life
in their hearts they began to twist the other growing nuts
from their stalks, so that in a short time they had collected
as many as they could control in their precarious position.

And the dry land *was* appearing. So they dropped their

39

nuts into the water and headed them towards the hump of land which they had left but an hour before. Their spirits were now as high as a little while earlier they had been low. The trees seemed to draw their trunks farther and farther out of the water. Big flat leaves of the undergrowth began to float on the surface, and then the grass appeared. The water was draining off quickly.

"What's that splashing? Why, fish!" Fish, indeed, which had come in with the big wave, and had been left as the water receded.

They caught as many of them as they could, and put them on the high ground with their store of coconuts. "We'll call this Three Palm Fort," said Patrick.

"Why fort?" asked Penelope.

"Well, it's the highest land and we must fortify it."

"Who are we going to fortify it against—sharks in the next flood?" Penelope wanted to know.

"No, savages from other islands—in war canoes."

"Rubbish!"

"Anyway, I'm hungry," said Patrick.

"So am I!"

Now came the problem: how to cook the fish? They had no possible way of making a fire. And how were they to open the coconuts?

"Let's get my knife," said Patrick.

"Your knife?"

"Yes, with my trousers, in my belt—back on the beach where we landed. Come on, let's find our clothes."

"Which way?"

"Blowed if I know; down there, I think."

Penelope turned and looked where he was pointing. She shook her head doubtfully. But Patrick had already started down the slope.

In their early morning stampede they hadn't bothered about landmarks, and, having reached the shore, they found something very different from what they had expected. Instead of their clothes they came on the remains of a hut made of palm leaves. "*Niau* house," said Patrick, having learnt the name in Tahiti.

Close to the hut and wedged between two trees was a four-legged stool which had a flat piece of iron like a blunt chisel attached to one end of it, for grating coconuts; and close by, stuck into the ground, was an iron spike for splitting the husks of the nuts.

At first they were afraid to look inside the tumble-down house, lest they should find the drowned body of its owner pinioned under the debris, but soon their curiosity overcame them, and they peered through the bamboo sides. It was obvious that someone had been living there till quite recently, but it was equally obvious that the owner was not there now. They could only suppose that he had been caught in the wave and drowned, and that his body was floating about the Pacific, if, indeed, it had not already been devoured by sharks.

Inside the hut they found a spear, a coil of rope, and a number of empty oyster shells.

This hut, however derelict it might be, gave a human air to the place, and Penelope suddenly became aware of her scanty clothing.

As they wandered along the shore hoping to reach the spot where they had slept, Patrick suddenly clutched her arm. "There's a flag," he said, "there, on that tree. Someone is about."

Dashing for cover among the near-by shrubs, they waited, hoping to discover who the intruder might be and what was the meaning of his signal.

41

"It's white," whispered Penelope. "That means peace."

"Keep quiet," muttered her brother. "You can't trust savages."

Their nerves were on edge, and they were thoroughly tired; furthermore they had had no food. When a fish flapped in a drying pool beside them they both nearly jumped out of their skins. When an overripe coconut fell with a crash they both dropped flat on the ground.

"Let's creep on," said Penelope, "and see who it is." So, on hands and knees, they picked their way through the thorny grass. After fifty yards or more Penelope stood up.

"It's still there," she said.

"Lie down," said Patrick, "and I'll creep on. Don't move unless I shout."

He was thin and wiry, and he made less noise as he moved alone. Emerging from the undergrowth, just opposite the pass in the reef, he jumped to his feet, waving and dancing on the sand, and shouting to Penelope to join him.

"What is it?" she asked. "Is it Uncle John?"

"No," he said, "it isn't; it's your vest."

Sure enough, the flood had left it hanging on a tree, for all the world like a signal of distress. Her skirt they found dragged half-way down a crab hole and badly chewed,

Patrick's shorts with belt and knife were almost where he had left them, and one by one they retrieved the rest of their clothes.

"Oh Lord, I *am* hungry," said Patrick. "Can't we get some food?"

Instead of returning by the beach they followed the line of their morning's flight, which led them back to their coconuts and fish. There was nothing much of interest on the way except a stunted lime tree.

"Good enough," said Penelope, picking some of the fruit. "Now we can cook our fish native fashion."

On reaching their store of nuts, they carried them to the hut where, with Patrick's knife, Penelope proceeded to clean the fish and scrape off the scales. Then she took out the bones and, cutting the flesh into small pieces, put them into a large empty coconut shell which she had found, and left them to soak in freshly squeezed lime juice, just as she had seen the natives do in Tahiti.

Meanwhile, Patrick was trying to open a nut by bashing it against the iron spike, but it is one thing to see an expert perform and another to do the job yourself. The nut skidded this way, it skidded that, it stuck on the spike, it slipped out of his hands and rolled down the slope before him; but

43

eventually it split and holes were bored through two of the three dark patches that are found at one end of a coconut. Some white people think that those three spots look like the two eyes and the mouth of a monkey, but the natives of the South Sea Islands think that that end of the nut looks more like the head of an eel, and they will tell you a fairy story of how the first coconut tree grew from the buried head of an eel.

The milk was cool and refreshing to drink, and the children began to feel better. Then they broke open the shell and scraped out the soft white flesh with their fingers.

"Always thought coconut was hard," said Patrick.

"It is at home."

"This is more like thick cream."

"Tastes better too," said Penelope, licking her fingers.

"What about that fish? Isn't it ready to eat yet?"

"It's still a bit blue," she said, stirring it with her finger in the lime juice.

"What are we going to live on?" asked Patrick.

"Blowed if I know."

Then they discussed how long they would have to wait before they were found. Would they *ever* be found? That was the question. When would Amundsen come back? And what had happened to Uncle John? Finally Patrick, mindful of his hunger, enquired again how the fish was getting on in the lime juice.

"Seems all right now," said Penelope.

In ten minutes' time there wasn't as much left as would feed a small flea.

"Gosh," said Patrick, "I'd never have thought it. It's better than fried any day. I tell you what, we'll try that spear, catch some more, then we're O.K."

"There must be other things," said Penelope. "Can't we find some breadfruit?"

"Tommy said they didn't grow on the small islands, they want deep soil or something; he said all these islands are made of coral with only a few dead leaves on top."

"Oh, I know," said Penelope crossly, "I heard them talking: only the seeds that float get carried here, and only the trees that can grow in the coral live—well, there seems plenty here, anyway."

"What is there?"

"Coconuts and—limes."

"Yes, a few on one tree. What else?"

"There's a lot of grass."

"We're not cows, are we?"

"There must be other things, somebody was living here before—"

"Come on, let's explore. Bags I the spear."

The sun was blazing hot, and as they wandered along they dipped their heads in the lagoon to cool themselves. The water was not more than a few feet deep and out of the clean sand at the bottom grew giant fingers of coral and large coral mushrooms, too, purple, emerald and cream. Penelope waded in. "Come quickly," she cried. "Oh, they're gone . . . no, they're not; look, there they go, thousands of them, bright blue."

"They're pink over here," called Patrick, "they're pink and green, if it's the fish you mean, and there's lots more with black and white stripes like zebras."

"Do come quickly," she said, "there's a huge one with a bright orange fin."

Patrick joined her and they sat down on a protruding rock to watch. They had once thought that the tropical fish in the London Aquarium were brightly coloured, but

45

the creatures that now surrounded them were so brilliant that anything they had ever seen before was pale in comparison. Penelope was entranced, but Patrick was all the time thinking of the possibility of food supplies. Once or twice he raised the spear to throw it but no sooner did he move than every fish in the place was gone.

"Have to make a trap," he said, "like that one at Tahiti. We must build up stones into a dam and drive the fish into a pool: then we can spear'em easy enough."

Along the north shore there was nothing but chunks of dead coral by the water's edge, and inland a thick plantation of coconut trees growing out of coarse grass.

"Not much food hereabouts," said Penelope.

"That coral would be good for the dam," said Patrick. "Let's cut across and see what we can find inside. What we want is a few logs to make a raft; then we could get down to the other islands."

"Get down a shark's neck more likely," said Penelope. "Old Amundsen says they attack canoes up here."

"Why don't they do it in Tahiti? What about all those people bathing near the town? Plenty of sharks in the lagoon there and they never touch anyone."

"Dunno, it's different down there, p'raps they're too well fed, there's enough rubbish in the lagoon."

"If we could find an old canoe," he said, "we'd be all right."

"It would have floated away in the flood."

"Not if it was anchored."

"There's nothing here, anyway. Let's go inland."

Before they had penetrated very far they came on a path. To the right it seemed to lead towards their three-palm hill, but following it in the opposite direction they came through thick brushwood on to marshy ground.

Here were growing more of the large elephant-eared leaves they had seen on the other side of the island.

"It's taro," said Penelope.

"How do you know?"

"Saw it in Tahiti the day we drove round the island. You eat the root. Come on, give me the spear."

"What for?"

"To dig it up."

"No fear, you'll bust it.'

"Well, scratch away then, and I'll pull.'

"Heave — heave — gently — gent-ly — hea-ve! Got him!"

Penelope looked at the round pink root with interest. "Now, what do we do?"

"Leave it till we come back, then we'll wash it, scrape it and eat it."

"This *is* fun. Bet you there's tons of food if we look for it."

"Move on. Gosh! Look here—!"

Just beyond where they were standing was a clump of

banana trees, their long flat leaves tattered and torn by the wind, but out of the centres of most of them hung a long hank of fruit.

"I thought someone said nothing grew on coral."

"But there's good soil here."

"Not much."

"More than on the other side, anyway: it's quite high above the water."

"It wasn't this morning!"

"How are we going to reach the bananas?"

"Let me get on your back," said Penelope.

"No fear, you'd kill me."

"Well, you get on mine."

She bent down, as if for leap frog, and he climbed on top.

"Gosh! Your knees are bony."

"Stand still and don't wobble."

He stood up and grabbed at the bananas. He caught them, but in so doing he lost his balance and next moment he was dangling in the air, hanging on the end of the bunch. Before he knew where he was, he was lying on the flat of his back, hugging a hank of fruit.

"We've got them, anyway," he said, getting up and rubbing his behind. "Now let's eat some."

Having put this idea into practice, they went ahead, leaving the rest of the bananas with the taro, to be collected on their return. The path, however, soon faded out in a thorny scrub, much too uncomfortable for bare legs, and they were compelled to return. But on reaching their store of fruit they found that instead of being against the tree where it had been left, the bananas were lying across the path and a number of them had been gnawed.

"Must be monkeys about," said Patrick. "Let's sit down and watch."

The heat of the day, following on their recent adventures, made them so drowsy that first one and then the other dropped off to sleep. When they woke an hour later their bunch of fruit had disappeared completely.

"I wasn't asleep at all," said Patrick. "I was only dozing."

"I only shut my eyes for one minute," said Penelope.

"Well, they're gone, and if we want any more we'd better bring the rope from the hut and climb for them."

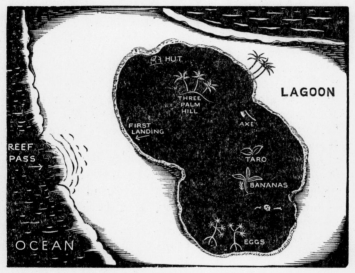

They got up rather wearily and followed the path back. After a short distance it branched to the right, and here they found themselves in a clearing in which were a series of shallow wooden trays fastened to stakes in the ground. In one of the trays was a long knife and, lying on the ground, a hatchet. As they were now quite sure that the

49

owner was not on the island, they took these with them and returned to the hut.

On getting back they opened another coconut, but instead of liquid there was nothing but hard and rather bitter white flesh; a second attempt produced the same result; only when they tried a young green nut did they find milk.

"All our fish have been taken," said Penelope, coming from the hut. "I left them under some leaves and every one has disappeared."

"It's those monkeys again," said Patrick.

"Where are they? Why haven't we seen any?"

"They must hide in the branches."

"Where's that taro?" continued Penelope.

"Just put it in the hut."

"Got to watch everything, seems to be plenty of food if we can keep it. What about a swim?" she said.

"Too tired, and it's pretty dark anyway. Where are we going to sleep?"

"Dunno! On the sand like last night?"

"No fear, might get caught in another wave."

"What about Three-palm hill?" suggested Penelope.

"Come on, let's go there now," said Patrick.

CHAPTER FOUR
MRS. BEETON BEATEN

"NO sign of a wave this morning," said Penelope, with a yawn.

"I wish there was some sign of breakfast," said Patrick.

"What is there?"

"Nothing!"

"That won't fatten us! What about bananas?"

"S'pose there's nothing else."

"Come on, let's get the rope," said Penelope, getting up.

"What for?" asked Patrick.

"To pull them down; you don't suppose you're getting on my back again?"

"Why not cut the tree down with the axe? They only fruit once—don't you remember what old Ebeneezer said in Jamaica?"

"I'd like porridge, eggs and bacon, some toast and butter and coffee."

"Don't talk rot. Are we going to live on bananas always?" he asked.

It certainly looked like it unless they could catch some fish. Patrick's idea of a dam grew more and more important. There were, of course, plenty of coconuts but, like the fish, they were difficult to get hold of. The young green nuts were all at the top of the trees; only the old dried husks lay about the ground. But if it came to the worst the whole tree could be cut down and then, besides getting the nuts, perhaps they could make a raft of the trunk.

As they went along they were followed by a number of

white gulls which were circling in the air and occasionally swooping through the trees, uttering raucous cries.

"They were there last night, too," said Penelope.

"There might be eggs. Gosh! Fish, eggs, fruit and vegetables and a house to live in."

"Half a house, and first catch your fish."

"Here are the bananas, which tree do you want?"

"They're nearly all unripe."

"They pick 'em green in Tahiti."

"That's no good to us, we can't wait for them to ripen. Here you are, slosh at it—wurrup—good—wurrup—good, another one—wurrup."

Suddenly the axe-head parted from the haft and went sailing into the bushes. Patrick followed it.

"Hoi, look at this!" he called.

He came back rather hurriedly.

"What's the matter?" asked Penelope.

"Bones! Lots of them, place is full of them."

"Rot!"

"I swear it," insisted Patrick.

"Got the axe-head?"

"Yes."

"Well, then, go on, cut the tree."

"The place is full of bones, I tell you, skulls and everything else."

He gave the tree another blow and it came scrunching to the ground.

"Do go and look," said Patrick; "they're human bones, I know."

"They can't be."

"They *are*."

Penelope peered through the bushes.

"Somebody must have died," she said.

"That's a bright remark," said Patrick; "there's two skulls there anyway."

"Well, I suppose they both died. There's a crack in one skull," she said, as she backed into the open.

"Let's go back to the hut," said Patrick, shouldering the bananas.

As they went along towards their hut, they felt uneasy about those skulls.

"They must have been there a long time," said Penelope, hopefully.

Patrick was less optimistic.

"Bones dry quick in the sun," he said.

They wondered if those bones were the result of a fight or the result of a feast. Mr. Pitcher had said that there were no cannibals on these islands, but perhaps he was wrong. Then they thought of the axe and the knife and the wooden tables, and they felt more gloomy than ever. But Penelope remembered that she had seen trays of coconut flesh spread out to dry in Tahiti, for copra. That raised their spirits a little. The axe might well be for splitting the nuts. They decided to hope for the best.

"You're right," said Patrick a little later. "I 'spect those bones have been there years and years, two chiefs fighting for the island like King Arthur and somebody or other his cousin, and they both did themselves in. That's what happened."

"They may have been fighting for a girl."

"Ohee, yaas!" said Patrick, scornfully. "Here, what about that dam?"

"The dam' what?"

"Shut up! I mean the trap for the fish."

"If only we could chase a few of them into one of those pools," he said, as they reached the shore, "and keep them there till the tide goes down, we'd have some chance of catching them."

"We never could."

"We might with a weir."

"Take us years," said Penelope.

"I'm going to try with the spear," said Patrick, "in deep water."

They climbed from chunk to chunk of the coral until they were half-way across the lagoon; but this was the limit of their advance, for here it sloped away steeply and the shallow pools were replaced by a deep current.

Fish of all kinds were passing along with the incoming tide. In particular there were shoals of twenty or more, about a foot in length, with speckled backs and scarlet tummies. There were others of about the same size which Patrick named the footballers, for from nose to tail they sported parallel stripes of the most vivid colours that an artist could squeeze out of a tube. Another variety had

54

a large black spot, like an extra eye, near the tail, so that they seemed to be swimming backwards, and some were all black and had flowing tails like a swallow, and others were divided in two with their heads of one colour and their tails of another. As Penelope sat with her feet in the water, all kinds of gay atoms came and nibbled at her toes.

But food was the all-important question. Patrick stood and heaved the spear into a shoal moving near the surface. He watched for the weapon to float again, and fully expected to see it dashing about in the water with one or more fish impaled. What actually happened was that he missed all the fish by yards, and the spear, instead of floating to the surface, lay peacefully at the bottom.

"Missed! Gosh, it's sunk, got to dive for it now."

"Go on," said Penelope.

He went in head first and swam till he thought he'd bust, but without success.

Then Penelope tried, with no better results. "It's miles deeper than it looks," she said.

"I'm going in like the natives," said Patrick, and, holding his nose, he took a mighty leap feet first. Down he went and his feet almost touched sand, but when he tried to double up and catch the spear he shot to the surface like a cork. The water was deeper than it appeared.

Penelope was dancing with excitement. "If you can do that again," she called, "we can catch heaps."

"Do what again?"

"Go in with a splash; all the fish shoot behind that rock over there and dodge out through the narrow pass beyond. We'll block that up and then we'll have them cold."

"We can't get on without that spear," said Patrick.

"We'll get it easier when the tide is low—better have a go at the house."

55

Patrick wasn't in the least interested in this idea, but a suggestion that they should look for eggs met with instant approval. Penelope wondered if they would find any more bones.

"Oh, shut up," said Patrick, "they've been dead for years —but," he added, thoughtfully, "I think I'll fetch the axe in case we want to chop anything."

"You know," said Penelope, "those monkeys were at our bananas in the night, several of them were gnawed."

"Wish we could see the blighters, might get 'em to throw nuts at us like they did in the *Swiss Family Robinson*."

"That's all a yarn," said Penelope.

"Bet you it isn't."

"Bet you it is."

Instead of taking the path through the taro patch, they followed the north line of the shore until it swung into a small bay almost immediately behind the higher ground which they had explored on the evening before.

Their arrival was greeted with a terrific hullabaloo of squeaks and squawks from several white terns which rose from the marshy land ahead. Circling about in the most alarming way, these small gulls swooped through the trees, soared into the air, then shot straight at the children's heads, only turning aside at the last moment.

Patrick swung his axe in the air for protection as they advanced towards a patch of scrub, and there in a hollow scraped in the sand they found one speckled egg. Every bird on the island seemed to screech at him as he picked it up. "Funny there's only one," he said as they took cover under a pandanus tree.

"S'pose the rest were carried away in the flood."

"Well, at all events it's fresh."

All this time the birds were skimming overhead, darting up and down and making the most terrific din. Not until the intruders had put a considerable distance behind them was there any sign of quiet.

"Those pandanus leaves are what they use for making hats," said Penelope. "I saw an old woman in Tahiti spliting them with a pin."

"Amundsen had a club which he said was made from one of the roots."

"You mean the branches that stick down?"

"They're not branches, they're roots, they grow into the ground. He says the natives cut off a bit of the tree as the head of the club and use the root as a handle."

"Sounds easy but I bet it's difficult."

"We'll try one day. How do we cook the egg?"

"I dunno!"

"Can't eat it raw."

"Well, we'll beat it up with coconut milk and make an egg flip."

"But what can we flip it in?"

"Empty coconut: use a few sticks for a whisk."

"We've got that taro to scrape too. A two-course lunch; we're getting on!"

Penelope was doing her best with the egg while Patrick took the taro root down to the water's edge to scrub.

He came back in a few minutes with his eyes and mouth screwed up, and making the most hideous faces. "Tastes like acid," he said.

"Must want cooking," suggested Penelope.

"My mouth wants washing."

"Try this," she said, handing him her concoction of egg. "Here! Steady on, don't finish it."

"Sorry, my gums are still sore."

"Look here," he said, picking a couple of bananas from the bunch, "we've got to get that spear."

"It's no good trying now," said Penelope, "the tide is too high; why is it always high here at midday?"

"Blowed if I know, s'pose it's different in the tropics," said Patrick.

"Must have a go for it this evening."

"But I'm *hungry*, I want some *fish*; let's try now, it may have moved."

No, the spear hadn't moved, it was exactly where it had fallen, and repeated dives failed to touch it. Then Penelope had a bright idea. She took off her skirt and tied it into a knot at the waist and filled it with stones. Holding on to this weight, she clambered into the water up to her neck, took a deep breath, put her head down and went straight

to the bottom. Catching the spear and dropping the bag of stones, she turned right way up, gave the sand a kick, and came to the surface as quickly as she had gone down.

Patrick was delighted. "But where's your skirt?"

"Oh! I never thought of that," she said, "it was pretty holey anyway. I'll have to wear leaves."

"Your pants are no worse than mine," he replied.

"That doesn't say much for them," said Penelope.

"Now for some fish," said Patrick. "What ho! I think we'll keep to the pools and just prod them. Stand by to catch as I throw them out. There's a big one! Ah, missed him, wait a mo'—there he is again. Gone! They're quick, aren't they? There's another. Phew, they do go a lick."

"Aim ahead of them," said Penelope.

"Not when they're still."

"Try it."

Splosh.

"Miles away—the water does something to the spear."

"Practise on a stone."

"All right—watch! See that white shell—now!"

But he was too much in front. Once again he tried with no better result. Then he aimed behind the mark and hit it.

"It's the water twists things," he said; "believe we had something about it at school—reflection or refraction or—there's a big one! Wait! Here goes—missed him."

"He moved," said Penelope.

"He's still there. Wait, wait. *Now! Got him!*"

"Don't let him off, keep your spear down. Is the point through him?"

"It's in the sand the other side."

"Scrape it up the rock and I'll get my hat under him."

"It's coming, it's coming, are you ready? He's a beauty; get the hat right round; all clear? Hooray."

Penelope lifted her hat clear of the water, with the struggling fish safely inside it.

"He's jumping like anything," she said. "Oh, the poor thing, can't you hit him on the head with a stone?"

"Keep him tight and let's get ashore first."

Penelope turned to follow Patrick, but her foot seemed to be stuck and try as she would she could not free it.

"I can't move!" she said. "Something's got my foot."

Patrick climbed across to where she was standing and peered into the water. He could see the tip of Penelope's shoe held between the two edges of a large shell, a shell rather like an enormous cockle.

"Wait a sec., you've trod on a clam. If I can get this

spear into him . . . Is that your foot?" he asked, probing inside the shell with his spear.

"Go on, go on, you're not touching me."

Patrick drove the spear deep into the clam, wrenching it from side to side.

"That's done it!" said Penelope, hopping clear. "Oo, my poor toes!"

"Seems to me you're lucky to have any left," said Patrick.

CHAPTER FIVE

PETTICOATS AND PIES

"ONE thing about this life," said Penelope next morning, "is that there's no bedmaking and mighty little washing up."

"I wouldn't mind a lot of washing up if there was a bit more to eat," said Patrick; "what I want is liver and bacon followed by steak and kidney pudding, and I wouldn't mind a loaf of bread, strawberry jam and a pot of tea."

"There were awfully few limes left on that tree last night," said Penelope; "we'll soon be eating our fish raw."

"If only we could make a fire," said Patrick.

"No good, can't do it, I've tried often, rubbing one stick against another. The only thing that gets hot is yourself. It takes a native: they know the kind of wood to use."

"If Uncle was here, he'd probably have a magnifying glass."

"He'd probably have matches."

"Couldn't even cook a bird if we caught one," said Patrick mournfully.

"We *ought* to be living on turtle soup and roast goat and guinea fowl," said Penelope.

They went along to where the terns nested, in hopes of finding another egg, and once again there was pillamaloo and hullabaloo and screeching and yauping, as the nesting site was invaded. This time they found three holes scratched in the sand with one egg in each but, by the time they had collected these, the attitude of the birds had become so threatening that they were compelled to beat a hasty retreat.

On the way home Penelope's mind ran on dressmaking and she picked a banana leaf with the idea of making a skirt, but when she tried to tie it round her waist it cracked and split and proved itself utterly useless for the purpose.

"Can't see why on earth you want a skirt," said Patrick.

"Supposing somebody comes?" she said.

"If anyone does we'll jolly well hide and keep quiet til! we see who they are."

"I'd have to wear more than this whether we liked them or not."

"Well, try the pandanus leaves, that's what they use for thatch."

"What are we going to do with these eggs?" she said, changing the subject.

"Another flip, I suppose."

Then she had an idea. Why not mash them up with bananas? Yes, it sounded good. Ten minutes later they tried it, and it *was* good.

Later in the day they tackled the hut. It seemed that the roof had rested on the sides, chiefly through its own weight, and having been bodily lifted by the flood had been let down again, anywhere but on its supports. Penelope had screwed herself inside with an idea of pushing it all up from underneath. Patrick at the same time had thought it wise to cut some of the lashings; the result was that whereas it had been only half down before, it was now completely collapsed and Penelope was underneath.

"Where are you?" called Patrick, as the fallen thatch heaved like an ocean swell.

"I'm here," she said, "squashed flat."

63

"Take more than coconut leaves to do that!" he said, rudely.

"Help me out," she called.

"Come on, what's stopping you!"

He was lifting the ridge pole to let her escape.

"I'm caught," she said, "in a net."

"Nonsense! Come on out, my arm is getting tired."

"I can't get out, I tell you; I'm tangled up in a net."

"All right, wait a while till I cut more lashings."

He chopped away at the cords which bound the various rafters, and in a few moments Penelope pushed her way through. Over her head, and down to her feet, was a net.

"For heaven's sake don't tear it," said Patrick excitedly, as he helped to extricate her.

"It must have been hanging under the roof," she said. "It just dropped over my head. Bit of a find, isn't it?"

Free of the thatch, the framework of the hut was simple enough. The ridge pole had rested in notches cut in the top of the end posts, just as the main rafters fitted on the side posts. Fastened to these at intervals were rods sloping to the ridge, where they were again made fast with strips of bark.

All this was easy to reconstruct, and it only remained to renew the lashings and tie on the palm leaves; but the old bark was now dry and brittle, and the one piece of rope on the island couldn't be spared.

This brought operations to a halt.

"Let's go and find some fresh bark," said Patrick.

"There isn't any," said Penelope, "there's only palms and pandanus, and they're no good."

"What about the hibiscus, those shrubs with the red flowers?"

"Let's try 'em," said Penelope.

64

On the morning after their first landing, when they had hidden in the bushes, they hadn't bothered about flowers; they were much too scared. But now they found a profusion of scarlet and crimson blossoms. Penelope picked one and put it in her hair.

"Don't be an ass," said Patrick. "You look like a native."

"Wish I was one," she replied, "then I'd know how to make fire and climb for nuts."

Patrick began cutting the bark and pulling it away in strips. Penelope did the same, and soon there was a pile of it on the ground beside them.

"I hope it's the right stuff," he said.

"It must be," said Penelope. "It's used in the hut and there's nothing else on the island."

When they got back it didn't take long to repair the framework, but a different problem arose when they came to tie on the thatch. Many of the plaited mats had come undone and it was no easy matter to get the hang of their construction.

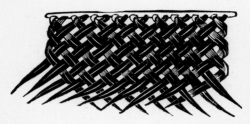

Patrick was inside shouting for more, Penelope was outside trying to fold the leaflets back into their old position. She discovered that each mat was the half section of a frond, split down the mid-rib and having the frondlets

C*

interlaced to form chequerwork. At each end these frond-lets were twisted back so that the ends were square. Once this was complete it was easy enough to lay them on the roof, one overlapping the other and fastened to the rafters with bark.

After a while they had had enough of this work.

"Too hot," said Patrick. "Let's have a rest."

"I'm going to make a skirt; where's that rope?" said Penelope.

"For heaven's sake don't waste it on that."

"Only a couple of feet."

"A couple of yards, more like."

"Shut up, skinny—I'm going along to the pandanus trees."

"I'm going to sleep," said Patrick.

An hour or so later Patrick woke up and yawned. "Gosh, you do look native," he said.

"But I can't sit down, they're too prickly," said Penelope. She had fastened the leaves along the rope and wound them round her body.

"Better go in the water and soften them; it's time for a swim anyway," said her brother.

"Let's take the net and see what we can catch," said Penelope.

The tide was almost at its lowest and they had a good opportunity of studying the contours of the rocks. They remembered how the fish had been turned aside by Patrick's splashing, and they now noticed that that particular channel, which at first wound its way through isolated lumps of coral, ended up in a fairly large pool from which there was but one outlet. If they could pin the net in that opening, and Patrick could continue his splashing in mid-channel, there was every chance that they would frighten some fish into the trap.

They began, then, to carry lumps of coral from the shore in order to block up the space around the open mouth of the net. But coral is heavy and it takes a mighty lot to make even a small dam, so that it was already growing dark before the work was finished.

During the day the south-easterly trade wind brings a breeze to all those islands in the south Pacific, but in the early morning and again in the evening the air is calm and the unruffled water of the lagoon becomes one vast mirror for the rising and setting sun.

"I've never seen such sunsets," said Penelope.

"I've never been so hungry," said Patrick.

They returned to the hut and settled themselves to sleep under their half-finished roof.

"I wish we had some roast beef," said Patrick.

"Or chicken, or turkey," suggested Penelope.

"With sausages and celery and roast potatoes."

"And dumplings . . . Let's go to sleep."

They settled down as if for sleep.

"I'd like one of Aunt Elisabeth's pies," said Penelope a few moments later.

"And a jolly good pudding like we used to get at Box Farm," muttered Patrick, half asleep.

"Good night," said Penelope.

"And chocolate ices and cheese," said Patrick, waking up again.

"I wish Granny was here—we wouldn't have to worry about anything."

They lay silent for a moment, and then in the stillness came a sound as of a mighty aeroplane. Ping! A large mosquito buried itself in Penelope's ear. At the same moment two more attacked Patrick. Then another and another joined the party; the hut began to sound like an electric power station.

"Come on," said Patrick, "let's go and sleep on the shore. I can't stand these mosquitoes."

They got up rather wearily and made their way to the edge of the lagoon. There were no mosquitoes there, and the sand was soft and warm. They soon wriggled holes in it for their hips, and in a few moments were sound asleep.

CHAPTER SIX

A WEIRD WEIR

"WILL you have your eggs boiled or fried, sir?" asked Penelope next morning, "or would you rather have them poached on toast?"

Patrick grunted; he was never at his best before breakfast and just then he was wondering where Amundsen was and why he had not come back to fetch them. He was feeling pretty dismal, too, about Uncle John who had not turned up.

"Must get some fresh coconuts today," said Penelope, "can't we climb one of the sloping trees?"

"Let's have some blinking bananas first," growled Patrick.

At one point of the coast there were four palms leaning over the lagoon and all of them bore fruit.

"We might reach those," murmured Patrick, "if we had anything to hold on to."

"Go on, sit on the tree and pull yourself up by your hands. I'll swim out and catch the nuts."

"How deep is it if I drop?"

"Plenty to catch *you*," called Penelope, wading in above her waist.

Patrick's progress was easy enough until the trunk turned upwards towards its head.

"Worse than the riding school," he said; "saddle's more slippery and no reins."

"Dig your knees in!"

"Wish I'd brought the rope; I could leave it hanging for another time."

"You're nearly there."

"It's darned spiky," complained Patrick.

"Get those green ones just above your head. Good! Let it go." Splash. "Another one!" Splash. "Splendid. There's two more on your right, can't you reach them? What's the matter? What are you looking at?"

"Get ashore," shouted Patrick, "get ashore quickly, there's a shark, he's quite close. For heaven's sake, hurry!"

Dropping the nuts, Penelope clambered out of the water. Yes, there he was like a great black shadow, his fin cutting the surface as he slid stealthily along. Patrick was clinging tightly to the tree, afraid to move lest he should slip. The shark was circling below as if expecting something to drop.

"Can't you drive him off," he cried. "Throw stones or something."

Penelope let fly a lump of coral.

Instead of being frightened the creature rushed to investigate the splash.

"Throw another farther away," cried Patrick.

Again the shark followed it.

Now she picked up a rotting coconut and a broken frond, each of which was enough to attract its attention. Meanwhile Patrick was skidding down the tree, leaving most of his shorts behind him.

"What next?" he said, puffing. "We've lost the blooming nuts."

Things were not so bad, however, for what little wind there was brought the nuts to shore. These they collected and took with them to the hut to crack open on the spike. Then, having finished a very dull meal, Penelope suggested finishing the dam.

"And get caught by the shark?" said Patrick.

"It's too shallow round there."

"Not where I jump."

"We'll easily see him."

"Will we? See inside p'raps—it's all right for you on the rocks." However, they decided to continue with the work, and half an hour's building completed the dam. It only remained to fix the net.

"Now you go across and splash," said Penelope, "and I'll climb out to the point and watch where they go."

"Oho! Nice little swim for me. Supposing that shark comes along?"

71

"It's only a few yards."

"Don't you think you'd make a much bigger splash?" asked Patrick.

"I'll go if you like," said Penelope.

"No, you won't!"

"All right, I'll watch for you. Go ahead."

He was across that channel in record time. "Seen anything?" he puffed.

"I don't think they'd come in so close," she said.

"Supposing they do, do I camp here?"

"Stay there now till I get back a bit. You say when," said Penelope, taking up a position between two large boulders.

"There's lots of small fish," called Patrick, "shoals of them."

"They're no good."

"The tide's wrong."

"No it isn't, it's coming in."

"Here they are then," shouted Patrick, leaping and splashing in the water.

The fish scattered and charged past Penelope, but instead of going into the net they dodged between the rocks and escaped.

"Do it again," she called, "do it again and I'll stop them here."

But they were too quick for her, and no matter how she jumped from stone to stone they always got through. "Hang your skirt across; it wants another soaking," called Patrick.

Next time he jumped, the startled fish went straight into the gully prepared for them, past Penelope's skirt of leaves, past her kicking legs, and through the narrows straight into the net.

"Come on," she shouted, "they're in."

She dashed after them, splashing for all she was worth. She tripped over a stone and splashed even more before she got on her feet again. Then she stood still and rubbed her eyes. A brown figure in a scarlet loin cloth was standing on the shore.

"You catching plenty fish?" he asked.

CHAPTER SEVEN

PAHEERO

"WHAT you doing on my island anyway?" said the stranger.

Penelope had got back to her skirt which she was trying to put on under water, and Patrick had joined her.

Before them stood this tall chocolate-coloured figure with a wreath of white blossom in his straight black hair. One eye drooped and a front tooth was missing, but otherwise, he might have been considered good-looking, for his features were regular and finely cut.

"What you doing here?" he repeated. "Where you boys come from?"

"England," said Patrick.

"Whar's you yacht? You go back aboard you yacht, this no island for you. I come here live alone, I no want white folks messin' about."

"We're not messing about," said Patrick; "we're wrecked."

"Whar's you ship?"

"Gone away in the storm—the *Rupe*—Captain Amundsen wouldn't stay."

"How you get ashore?"

"He gave us the boat."

The stranger shook his head, disbelievingly.

"It's true," said Patrick.

"Whar's boat?"

"Wrecked—we never saw it after we upset. Our uncle is

74

gone too. We think he's drowned. Suppose you haven't seen him, have you?"

"What like is he?"

"Short," said Patrick.

"And bald, no hair," said Penelope.

"He's no drowned, he's on Hikueru."

"Where's that?"

"Down there, fifty miles," said the native pointing across the island.

"Have you seen him?" asked Penelope.

"No, I not seen him, schooner at Marama say him picked up in boat, at sea. He got broken leg and no paddles. They take him Hikueru."

"Can we get to Hikueru?"

"Yes, you get there quick enough on schooner."

"How quick?"

"One month, two month, p'raps three month—plenty schooners."

"I don't call that plenty, or quick," said Patrick.

Now that the owner of the island was reassured about the identity of his visitors, his manner changed.

"You sure you not picture folks?" he asked, "and you sure you not gadding folks off yacht? Then you stay along here, I take you Marama one day soon."

"Is there enough food for us?" asked Patrick.

"Food, *kai-kai*, plenty *kai-kai*, plenty fish, plenty *tupa*, plenty taro."

"What's *tupa*?"

"Crab—big coconut crab. They climb trees, eat nuts. We catch them, much fat, very good."

"Isn't there any meat?"

"*Puaka*, you call him pig—I bring two little *puaka* in

pirogue, what you call canoe. And I bring plenty *pisupo*—p'raps you call him *bullamacow*."

For some reason which no one seems to know, the name *pisupo* throughout all the eastern South Sea Islands means corned beef. One can only suppose that the first tinned food seen by the natives of these islands was pea soup, and therefore they thought the name applied to anything in a tin. Further to the west, the same tinned beef is known as *bullamacow*, because it was on one of those islands that Captain Cook left a bull and a cow from which all their cattle are descended and from which their beef has since been produced.

But at this juncture neither Patrick nor Penelope was thinking of the derivation of words.

"We're frightfully hungry," said Penelope.

"We have *kai-kai* mighty quick. You come with me," said the native.

"There's fish in our net," said Patrick.

"No fish in that net, they gone away home long while back. That net for little fish, you try catch 'em too big, parrot fish make mighty kick, net no more. You come with me, we go fetch food. Ah, you find my spear, he not swim away in flood? What else you find?"

"Nothing," said Patrick; "the house had fallen down."

"Yes! I know house fall down in flood, that's why I stay Marama till storm finish. How you like big wave? Not much I guess! We soon build new house. How you call yourself?"

"Patrick!"

"Pa-treek—Pa-treek. What that mean?"

"Don't know," said Patrick.

"And you other boy?"

"Penelope."

"Annellummy?"

"No! Pen-el-o-pee."

"Pen-lel-loppy, what that mean?"

"Don't know," said its owner, "what's your name?"

"Paheero!"

"What does that mean?"

"That says the fort of the mighty caterpillar."

"The what?"

"The fort of the mighty caterpillar."

"Gosh! Why that?"

"'Cause my father's father, him called Tepoto 'cause he small man, but him have very great friend, very long thin man, very big fighter. And my father's father he loved him very much, make him *tayo*, that is special friend. Then they give each other their own names, so my father's father he called 'home of the great caterpillar', and his long friend, very great warrior, called Tepoto, which is how you say 'the short'."

"Isn't it silly to change names?"

"Only great friends when they love each other."

"It seems *very* silly," remarked Penelope.

"But some day you love some man and you throw you name into sky and he give you his name."

"That's different," said Penelope.

"Only a little bit different, but sad for you, 'cause your name thrown away altogether, never anyone take care of it. In Tahiti we give our name to special friend, he take great care of it. He give his name to us, we take great care of it for him."

As they approached the shore, they could hear grunts and squeaks from two little pigs which were trussed up in the bottom of the canoe. Alongside them was a crate of chickens, a sack of sweet potatoes and a bundle of bamboos. In the stern were wooden cases and various tools and implements such as a new and shining adze, which Paheero explained was for making another canoe. A few years earlier the head of the adze would have been of stone: now it was of bright steel and sharp as a hatchet; but with the blade at right angles to the handle instead of parallel to it. In many parts of Europe today the very same tool is used for boat-building.

While Patrick was admiring the tools, Penelope seized one of the pigs, not much bigger than a rabbit, and was just about to let it loose when Paheero restrained her. "You tie him one leg to tree," he said; "I show you—now same thing along this boy," and he picked up the other pig.

Meanwhile Patrick had spotted the wooden cases, which suggested food, and was about to lift one of them to carry it to the hut.

"You leave that box, I carry him myself," said Paheero, hurriedly.

"What's in them?" asked Patrick.

"Nothing in them—they just full o' sand for balance *pirogue*. You leave them in *pirogue*. I come back one time, throw him away. Now we go make *kai-kai*."

At the hut they found two big tins of fresh water, already dumped there by Paheero.

"Is that *real* water, for drinking?"

"Huh! You like some?"

He gave them each a coconut shell full.

"What you drink, *les cocos*?" he asked.

"Coconuts, yes! We're sick of them," said Patrick.

"And you eat *les bananes*?"

"Yes!" said Penelope, "and eggs and nuts."

"The taro is awful," said Patrick.

"How you cook him?"

"We didn't, we tried it raw."

"Oo la-la, he bite tongue, if you not cook him he tie up teeth, stick pins in gums."

Paheero was now busy preparing a native oven, called by him an *umu*. Having scooped a hollow in the sand, he piled up in the centre of it all the dry sticks and timber that he could find. Then with a box of matches, from the folds of the brightly coloured cotton that he was wearing around his waist, a *pareu* he called it, he soon had a blazing fire, around and on top of which he laid stones. As the fire subsided the stones from the outer edge were moved in so that it became a glowing mass of wood and stone.

While this was going on, Penelope had been scraping the rind off the breadfruit and scrubbing the sweet potatoes. Patrick had gone to collect banana leaves, and Paheero during the intervals of fire-minding was carrying further sacks and boxes from the canoe.

After one somewhat lengthy absence he appeared with a long bundle wrapped in leaves. "*Puaka-iti*," he said, "*puaka* pig, *iti* little—one little pig, ready for *umu*."

"Poor little thing," said Penelope.

79

"No, he not poor any more time, he happy now. Other little pig sad, 'cause he left all alone, tied by leg."

On the arrival of Patrick, the hot stones were raked over to allow the ashes to fall through, and they were then covered with several thicknesses of leaves. On these the pig and the various bundles of breadfruit and potatoes were arranged, each in their green wrappings. More leaves were laid on top, more stones and again more leaves. Finally even the old fronds from the fallen roof were thrown on, to keep in the heat.

"I wish *we* had had matches," said Penelope.

"I show you how make fire one day," said Paheero.

"Two pieces of wood?"

"That's right; why you not make it?"

"Couldn't—I tried in Tahiti. Besides, everything was wet."

"D'you know why fire come out of wood?"

"Friction or something like that," suggested Patrick.

"No, that wrong, I tell you. Long time ago fire belong one man only in all world. One day son of his grandson ask him, give him fire. He say No! Next day son ask again, again old man say No! Next day after, he ask again, again he say No! Then son of his grandson angry, say, 'If you not give it, I take it'. Then old man hit young man. They begin fight—they fight long, many big blows. Then old man fall down, hit head very hard on rock, then fire in head jump out into rock; it jump into all trees, too. Then old man die."

"Is that why there's sparks in stone?" asked Patrick.

"That's him. If you want fire come out of stone, you hit very hard quick, like young man hit old man, then fire jump out. If you rub woods together, you rub like two men fight, quick, quick. But you must have hair of *niau* husk, like the hair of old man, then when you rub sticks, hot fire come in the hair. Why you not sit still, Annelopee?" he added. "I see you all time move about like you was sitting on centipede."

"It's this skirt," said Penelope; "it prickles."

"But why you wear *lauhala*? You must get *purau* bark. When we go cut trees for new house we put sticks soak in water. Then four, five days you pull bark off sticks and I show you how make dress. Now I lend you *pareu*."

Forthwith he produced from one of his sacks two yards of scarlet cotton, and in a few moments Penelope found the business of sitting down very much more comfortable.

"Now we go fetch coconuts," he said.

He led them to one of the hibiscus trees, from which he pulled a strip of bark about three feet long. Tying the two ends in a knot, he stopped under one of the tallest palms. Glancing up to make sure that the nuts were what he wanted, he put his left foot into one end of the loop, gave the bark a couple of twists around his instep and then put his right foot into the remaining stirrup. Before they had realized what he was doing he had shinned half-way up the tree, and a moment later he was calling to them to mind their heads as he sent the nuts hurtling down, with a peculiar spin so that they hit the ground on their pointed ends and did not split.

"Wish I could climb like that," said Patrick when Paheero had returned to earth.

"You white man, an' all white men too slow, too stupid. You never can climb tree 'cause you is white man, and you never can swim 'cause you is white man, but if you very quick white man p'raps you make fire one day."

"But we *can* swim," said Penelope.

"Yes! I see you in water. Make me laugh. I think I nearly call you *Rati-nui*, that mean, big splash."

"She got a prize for swimming at home," said Patrick rather indignantly.

"How long she swim for?"

"Half a mile."

"Half a mile!" Paheero roared with laughter. "Half a mile, she get big prize in Tuamotus I guess. You no hear of Tuamotu woman swim two whole days in storm with sick husband on back? Half a mile, half a mil.—now I know why white boys build big ships."

He was still chuckling when he reached the hut and began to split the husks of the nuts on the iron pin in the ground. One biff here and one biff there and the job was done. "Half a mile! Half a mile!" he kept chortling.

"Where's machete?" he asked, looking round for the long knife.

Two cuts an inch apart, and two more crossing them, made a neat hole. "Now you fetch salt water in shell—we mix him with the coconut milk and make sauce."

While Patrick was fetching the water Paheero began to remove the covering from the oven. "You spread clean leaves," he said to Penelope. "Little pig he goes here, *uru*, breadfruit, he goes here, *umara*, sweet potato, he goes here. Then we mix sauce an' we eat." He had unwrapped the breadfruit and sweet potatoes and laid them on either side of the main dish, and now he was severing the flesh from the pigling's bones.

"*Mangez lentement, mangez lentement*," he cried, as both the children fell on the food that was put before them. They were all eating with their fingers and he himself was dipping each mouthful in the sauce. The breadfruit in particular he broke into pieces and swallowed with loud sucking and squelching noises.

"You not like?" he asked. "You eat very sad, I not hear you like much."

Patrick at this moment gave a loud hiccup.

"Ah, you like! That good. When we hear noise in Tuamotus we know friends happy, when no noise we think they no like food."

He followed up his own remarks by a huge belch.

Patrick giggled. Penelope hid her smile and managed to look pained.

"Why you laugh, you white boy? Always you white men afraid show how you think. I eat with white man, Rarotonga, they always sad, no enjoy *kai-kai*."

83

Eventually there was nothing left but bones and empty leaves.

Paheero rolled all together and threw them aside. "Crabs soon clear up all that," he said. "Now we go little sleep."

"We can't think where the monkeys hide," said Patrick.

"Monkeys, monkeys? You bring monkeys on island?"

"No fear; they're here already."

"What you say? Monkeys here, here on island? No, I think you sit in sun too long."

"But they took our bananas," said Patrick.

"And fish," added Penelope.

"They not monkeys, they crabs," said Paheero. "Where you leave bananas? On ground? What you think, then— when big crab come along look, he say *tabu*, white man's *kai-kai*, go away again? No, not crab; crab have sense, him not native boy, kanaka, 'fraid white man. Him take what he find."

It must have been an hour later when Penelope awoke. Patrick also rubbed his eyes and sat up. With their tummies full, and good news of their uncle, the world seemed a very much brighter place.

"Allo! Allo! You boys, you wake up, you have nice sleep. I think I very glad you come to my island, you nice boys. We have good fun all together, before I take you Marama."

Paheero came striding towards them carrying two empty boxes, the same that had been in the stern of his canoe.

"I bring along boxes for new house, white ladies always like boxes, make tables, chairs. Yes, we build fine house. And I take you fishing—we catch flying fish—we catch octopus—we dive for pearl shell. I give you pearls, you give me shell."

84

Penelope opened her eyes. "You give us pearls?" she asked.

"Yes! I give you all pearls *you* catch, and you give me all shell you catch."

"Are there many pearls?"

"Not many pearls, not many shell; when you go Hikueru you find plenty pearls, plenty shell. Hikueru best island in all Tuamotus, divers go five hundred miles to Hikueru."

He went on to explain that they couldn't go diving until the *rahui*, or close season, was over. The French Government wouldn't let them fish for pearls all the year round because they said there would soon be no oysters left.

"How deep under water are the shell?" asked Penelope.

"Four, five, p'raps six metres you find small shell; big shell in big water. We go one day on lagoon when *rahui* finish."

Patrick was very anxious to borrow the canoe and explore the coast line but, for some reason or other, Paheero wouldn't hear of it.

"Tomorrow, not today, you take it. Now I go fetch more boxes, you stay here."

"Can't we help you?"

"No! I not want no help—you stay where you are. When the big chief Paheero say you stay here, then white boys stay here. I go fetch boxes, you stay here. If you like, you go swim."

So saying, he disappeared among the trees, leaving them to wonder why he would not lend the canoe and why he had refused their offer of help.

When they came back from the lagoon it was getting dark. Paheero had returned and was even more cheerful than before. "I like you boys very much, tomorrow we build fine house and we make dress for Ann-epoli. Yes, I very glad you boys come stay along of me."

He had brought with him some of the scarlet fruits of the pandanus trees and was weaving them into wreaths. "You wear these," he said, putting one on each of their heads, "and I make you Tuamotu music." He produced a bamboo flute and began to play by blowing into it with his nose. "This is song of Kina," he said. "Kina is little sea urchin. When there's big storm coming little Kina listens to roar of big waves, then he creeps into little hole, hides himself till sea all calm again. If we see Kina all gone from reef we know big storm coming. That song says: Listen Kina, listen Kina, for angry talk of big waves.

"Now I play you *I te are e huti, I te moana o Marama,* that is about the big waves that rise in the sea of the moon. This lagoon called Marama 'cause it is shape like the moon. We on one point here, fifteen miles over there is other point and big islands."

He continued to play, explaining each tune as he went along. There was the song of the handsome shark who loved the chief's daughter, and the eel who married the princess, and many others.

Suddenly he got up. "*Va poiri voa,*" he said, meaning: It is quite dark. "Good sleep, you boys." And next minute he was gone.

CHAPTER EIGHT

A LITTLE EDUCATION AND A
LARGE CRAB

"COME on, you white boys, you waste half day sleepin'—we build house today. Never can know why white man sleeps all day, wakes all night."

Paheero was opening a tin of beef with the axe.

"What time is it?" said Penelope, yawning.

"*Ua peretia te ra.*"

"What's that?"

"The sun, it spreads everywhere."

"Is it late?"

"Half-way to the high tide, time you boys dig holes, build house—but you white folk all same thing, sleep, sleep, sleep all morning, never see blue clouds fly away, never see red clouds come up over sea, never hear bird first sing, never hear flies make morning buzz."

"What time were you up?" asked Patrick.

"Time see man's face, time know one man's face from other man's face, sun down below sea."

"Can we have some of that beef?"

"Sure thing! I sell big pearl, buy plenty *pisupo*. You like salad too?"

"Salad?"

"Palm salad, that's how you call him. You eat," he said, offering them a shell full of crisp white flakes like chopped celery. "That is little top of coconut tree, I cut him this morning, make posts for house, now you have salad like white man Rarotonga. I live Rarotonga long while, that where I learn speak English. Now I go cut *purau* sticks. When you bellies full, you come along shore."

Half an hour later they found him tying the newly-cut rods into bundles. "You take these along banana trees, then I come put them soak in water."

He lifted a bundle of the twigs on to each of their shoulders and they staggered off.

It was all they could do to carry them.

"Mine's dropping," said Penelope, before they had gone a hundred yards.

"I'm dropping myself," said Patrick, "and my backbone is—cracking and—my shoulder—phew!"

"Stick it till we're round the corner, he's watching us."

They managed to keep going till out of sight, but after that they made a double journey of it, carrying one load between them each time. They were still puffing when Paheero arrived with a bundle of the heavy rods on each shoulder.

"Now we lay little sticks in water, few days' time make soft dress, an' we take big sticks along make house."

They picked their way across the stepping stones till they

came to a muddy pool, unoccupied by the taro, and in this they put the lighter twigs to soak.

"We come back five, six, seven days," said Paheero; "then we find sticks soft and we beat them, make Tuamotu dress, Annelummy."

He shouldered his bundles and strode ahead of them towards the hut. "I think we build house close by lagoon," he said; "then we not have *namu*."

"*Namu?*"

"Yes, *namu*, *moustiques*, what you say moskitto, they not like wind from sea. You stay here, I go fetch spade— Annelummy dig holes, Pa-treek he come carry *niau* posts."

Paheero returned in a few minutes, carrying a spade and crowbar.

"When I go Marama I put spade sleep deep in sand, tie him along of bar, he no swim, no two-legged crab find him, he quite safe. Now Nelopee, you dig mighty big hole here'bouts and when you finish, you dig 'nother mighty big hole there'bouts—you come with me, I show you," and he paced a dozen feet along the sand. "You go down long as you arm—Treeko an' me, we fetch posts."

Paheero led the way to the scene of his early morning activities, where the palm was lying, cut into lengths.

"This big fat end make fine *pirogue*," he said.

Near by was a pile of fronds trimmed for plaiting, and there was a collection of the fibrous sheaths which adhere to the base of the fronds as an extra attachment to the tree. These measured some eighteen inches across and their close and regular texture had all the appearance of hand weaving.

"Once on time they make sails, an' once on time they

D

make shirts," said Paheero. "Now Tuamotu men sell copra an' buy *pareu* in Papeete. Now you lift pole," he added. "You got him?"

"Y-es," said Patrick, rather doubtfully.

"And I lift this end and we go along fix in hole made by Nelopee. You mind where you walking," he said as Patrick stumbled over some nuts, "those green *oua* all on one side, they good drinking; brown *niaa* over there, they too old, they make copra and rope."

"Rope?"

"Yes, I show you one day, and oil. Say! Why you wobble? You keep out of lentana bush or you get mighty bad scratch."

"It's heavy," said Patrick.

"No, not heavy, but you walk all bent like crab's leg. All white men same thing, never can walk straight, never can carry one small coconut, all time say heavy, heavy. I think white man stay too long read books, all time tell other man how do something, himself do nothing."

"Can we rest?" said Patrick, panting.

"Yes, you put him down your end; I stand him up. If he stand straight, he hold all whole island on head; if he lean like palm tree, he not hold one little moskitto.

"Now you ready?—Not yet?—You know story Solomon Island man tell. He say when white man stop work, him say, 'cause he exhausted; when kanaka stop work, white man say, 'cause him dam' lazy."

"It's so hot," said Patrick.

"Treeko, you good boy," said Paheero. "You stay here with me, and I make you strong Tuamotu man and Nelopee I make her Tuamotu girl. Why you want go back home? I see white man in Papeete, all time sit in house read book, all time wear mishnary dress, all time white face like dead man, all time no hair on head, all time buy sell buy sell, all time not happy."

"I've got to earn money some day," said Patrick.

"Why you want money? If you look for money you never have some; if you not look for it, you have plenty always."

"Uncle says we've got to earn our living."

"Your uncle like all white men silly dam' fool. He want you want all things you not want. He want you sit in house all day till you behind so stiff you not able walk. Then you bang bell, someone bring you drink—then you bang bell, someone change you clothes—then you bang bell, someone make *kai-kai*. Then all you money gone, you sit in house all time next day."

"I'd stay if Penelope would," said Patrick.

"An' Nelopee say she stay if you stay. Now we go talk Nelopee, you hold your back straight like house post, now I lift other end. Good boy! Treeko, one day I make you big Tuamotu man."

Penelope was lying on her stomach by the water's edge and was so intent on the pool before her that she did not see the others return.

"Do come quickly," she called in answer to their shout.

"What's the matter?"

"A crab, a crab out of its shell, do look!" She held up a small trumpet shell.

"It was inside and it suddenly walked out and left the shell. When I put my hand in the water it ran back, but I got there first; now it's running round like mad trying to get into another, but they are all too small. Why hasn't it got its own shell?" she asked Paheero.

"Those fellows got no shell of own, they always go along other boys' shells; when they grow big, they change house,

91

find bigger shell. When you see him, he go look for new house, his belly grow too fat for this one."

All the time the little naked creature was dashing about, trying to insert the end of its tail into another shell, but anything of the right size was already occupied; finally, it hid itself in a crevice of the coral to wait for better luck with the incoming tide.

"Give him back his house," said Penelope to Paheero, who had taken it.

"No, I give him bigger," he said, picking one out of the shingle near by. "Now you watch, see."

He dropped the shell into the water close to the crab. There was a pause, two long eyes appeared, there was a quick sideways rush, and next minute the unhappy mite had buried itself tail first in its new abode.

"Those fellows too small, no good nothing," said Paheero. "Tonight we go catch big coconut crab. How far you dig holes?" he asked Penelope.

"Not far," she answered; "it's all rock."

"Well, why you not break up with bar? That's why I bring bar. You come see. That not rock, look see—look see," as he levered up the chunks of dead coral.

"Now Nelopee, you come Treeko and me, we carry back other pole all together. Treeko he say he stay this island if you stay. How you like stay, and I make you Tuamotu boys?"

"How about Uncle John?"

"Uncle, Uncle, always you say Uncle. I tell you he safe Hikueru, why always talk Uncle? If he want see you, he come schooner, plenty schooners come all time Hikueru."

"He wants us to help him."

"How you help him?"

"Catch fish for his book."

92

"Book? And how you catch fish anyway? I guess you catch lots fish 'fore I come along this island! Why he want fish for book?"

"To sell and make money, I suppose."

"Oh Ja-rooselem the golding! Why make the money? What for you want the money? I got no money, but I see plenty fish all day. I take you in *pirogue* one time, show you fish too smart ever make picture."

By this time they had reached the fallen tree.

"Now Treeko, you hold you back straight like I tell you. Nelopee, you must walk like if you carry egg on top of you head. Now we—lift post, and we—walk straight, and we get back along shore quick as crab into shell."

"I'm hungry," said Penelope, as they dropped the log on the beach.

"You hungry?"

"I am too," said Patrick.

"Huh! Then p'raps we done 'nuff work—what you think?"

In due course the old ashes in the oven were raked away, the stones relaid and the fire lit.

"I bring those stones from Marama," said Paheero; "coral no good for *umu*. You fire him one time, he no good no more. Now I think we go along catch fish." He picked up his spear and left them.

As he reached the edge of the lagoon his paces became slower. Almost crouching, he crept along, stepping quietly into the shallow water. His spear was now poised, its weight balanced in his left hand, while the first finger and thumb of his right hand against the butt of the weapon were ready to send it hurtling forward at the first sign of a fish. Cautiously he moved along, his eyes scanning the water all around him. Then, of a sudden he threw the spear. Neither Patrick nor Penelope had seen any indication of fish, but now the handle of the spear was waving about in the water and Paheero was striding forward. A moment later they saw him take a large fish from the point of the spear, bite its head to kill it, and then throw it ashore.

Again and again he threw the spear, and again and again a fish flopped on the ground beside the children.

"I think one day we make net, then you boys catch fish while I make new *pirogue*," said Paheero, as he came ashore. "Now we go home, and Nelopee scrape taro same like she scrape breadfruit. Treeko, you take fish, cut off heads, tails, wash guts; I go fetch leaves of *banane*."

He was some time away, but when he returned he brought not only the leaves for cooking but wreaths of hibiscus blossom for their heads. "If I make you Tuamotu boys, you always wear flowers at feast. Now we fix *umu*."

The fish and the taro were packed in leaves and placed on the hot stones, and more leaves and stones were added just as when they cooked the pig.

"Now Paheero go small walk, come back plenty time *kai-kai*."

"Can we come?" asked Patrick.

"You boys stop along here. Big chief Paheero not want no one along of him when he go walk, he back along soon."

"Can't think where he goes," said Patrick; "he slinks off and stays away an hour. He's done it several times."

Paheero was very much out of humour when he got back. "Say! Who's been messing about in *marae*?" he asked.

"In what?"

"*Marae*, that's holy place—someone's been poking in bushes along of bones."

"We were trying to get through," said Patrick.

"What for get through? You no want get through. *Tabu*! Don't you go touch nothing there. *Tabu*, all *tabu*."

"Whose bones are they?" asked Penelope.

"Bones very great chief, bones two very great chief, many great chief buried there—*tabu*!"

"We only looked through the bushes," said Patrick.

"That's all right, you go along no farther—don't you go along there no more—p'raps you get touching bones, then p'raps something bad happen you. I tell you *TABU*!"

An hour later the land crabs were scavenging the remains of the meal and Paheero was tying together a number of banana and coconut fronds. He had quite recovered from his ill humour.

"Tonight we go catch big coconut crab," he said, as he plastered the leaves with mud.

"Did they have a terrific battle?" asked Patrick; "the chiefs, I mean."

"Why for you ask?"

"'Cos one of them had a huge split in his skull."

"Huh, you see him—that great chief Arii-mao. You sure you not touch bones?"

"Couldn't get near them if we'd wanted to," said Penelope.

"That good thing for you; p'raps you go in there, mess about with bones, then one day you skin fall off or you eyes shut up dark."

"From just touching the bones?"

"From just walking about where *tabu* is."

When Paheero got up the children followed him to the new house, and watched while he deepened the holes begun earlier in the day by Penelope. Finally they held the posts upright for him while he filled in the soil and stamped it firm.

"Now I think we sit down, and we wait for the dark," he said, "and then we wait for the moon, and then . . . we wait for the crab."

"Is that really true about the bones?" asked Penelope.

"Course it's true, I'm not white man tell lies."

"But they're dead, they can't do you any harm."

"You think so? What happen Ellity along Raiatea?"

"Don't know," said Penelope.

"Don't know! I tell you quick enough. White man called Ellity think he have great fun take bones from *marae*. When priest say *tabu*, Ellity laugh. Then he go dig along *marae*, find skull mended with *niau* shell and put him in pocket. Priest very cross, he say *tabu tabu*. Then Ellity go along schooner. Priest say he not fetch up Papeete. Outside reef, strong wind strike ship, sail hit Ellity on head, he fall in water, sink, finish."

"Might have been an accident," said Patrick.

"*Tabu!*" said Paheero.

"Why was the skull mended with coconut shell?"

"*Niau* shell make mighty good bone, fix him in clean, bone grow alongside double quick."

"The man wouldn't live, would he?"

"Course he live, live long time; shell, bone, all fix together, skin grow, he very happy."

"Bet he had headaches," said Patrick.

"Then he go along *tahu'a-mori*."

"Where?"

"To doctor who rub oil in, p'raps he man, p'raps he woman. Old Vahine-moea she mighty good, she live Papeete; all white folk go along, she bang pain away, she . . ." Paheero suddenly stopped talking. "Ss-s-s," he whispered, "there's *kaveu*."

A falling coconut had been the only sound, yet its particular thud on the ground was sufficient to tell a trained ear that it was a young and succulent nut, not an old one; and there must be a reason for its fall.

Paheero knew the reason, and a faint grinding noise from the branches overhead reassured him. Climbing half-way up the tree, he wound his muddy leaves round and round the trunk so that they formed a band several inches thick.

"That all O.K.," he whispered. "Now we spread stones round roots, make nice soft cushion for old man crab."

The moon was lifting itself over the low palms and lighting up the stems of the taller trees when Paheero pointed upwards. A shadow was moving on the tree—lower and lower it came—till they could recognize the long arms of a crab descending, stern first.

When its tail made contact with Paheero's leaves it stopped a moment, as if to say: "This trip is shorter than I thought." Cautiously feeling about for a moment, it made sure that earth had been reached. Then it let go. Next moment there was a horrible scrunch on the stones below.

Paheero ran forward with a stick, but except for a twitching of the claws there was no sign of life in the crab.

"Tomorrow we eat him," he said. "Now I think we go along sleep."

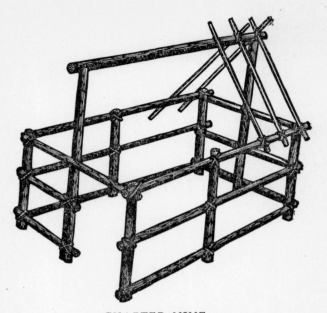

CHAPTER NINE

QUEER FISH AND QUEER STORIES

NEXT day they did eat the crab, and Paheero extracted a quantity of oil from a bag under its tail. "Mighty good for sick skin," he said, as he squeezed it into a coconut shell.

They also continued building operations. The ridge pole of the house was fitted, and four corner posts were stood in the ground. Midways on either side they put an extra one for strength, so that the ground plan showed a total of eight verticals. Allowing space for a door, they lashed three horizontal rods at each side, and the same at the ends.

"Now I go up top," said Paheero, climbing on to the ridge. "Treeko, you stand on box and Nelopee she give you bamboos. I fix him here, you fix him there. Where's that *purau* bark? That's him, nice and soft after been in water.

"Now you watch me, Treeko, see how I lash these boys tight, that's right, put him through there, now pull him tight. Good boy Treeko, when you arms tired, you give job Nelopee."

By midday they had completed one side of the roof.

"Tell us a story," said Penelope, as they were resting after their meal.

"Story?" asked Paheero.

"Yes, something queer—about the Islands."

"Nothing queer about the Islands. Only queer things I know—about white men."

"Us!" exclaimed Patrick.

"All white men same thing, tell lies, 'spect Tuamotu boys swallow nonsense."

"We haven't told you lies."

"No, not yet you haven't, you good boys; when you been in island while longer then you tell plenty lies, p'raps you begin tell story like white captain Papeete. He say white man Londoni walk quicker than motor car. Yes, he say that. I say no! I seen motor car Tahiti, I seen white man Tahiti. Motor car taxi go bang-bang-pfut-speeze, and he round island double quick. White man walk across road once twice, he tired, very tired, must have drink, must have sleep."

"Need we do any more on the house today?" asked Patrick.

"Huh! I think you want go sleep too."

"I want to go on the lagoon," said Penelope.

101

"What for, see fish make book for uncle? Come along, I take you."

They launched the canoe and paddled away to the south. Penelope knelt in the bow, Paheero sat amidships with the paddle and Patrick sat in the stern.

The water on their left towards the break in the reef was deep and clear, but on their right they skirted coral ledges of strange and fantastic formation.

"Like great cabbages and cauliflowers," said Patrick.

"Dahlias and begonias," said Penelope.

There were growths resembling huge plates, and others on stalks like giant mushrooms; some were speckled and looked soft like an uncooked plum pudding, and others had all the delicacy of the skeleton leaves you find in the English woods in winter. In and about this underwater garden were myriads of fish. Every yard of the coral was different and every foot of it held something new.

Gliding into a shallow patch, the canoe grated on a bed of the pink stagshorn variety.

"Stuck," said Penelope.

Paheero stood up and rocked the canoe backwards and forwards. The brittle growth beneath them cracked. One stroke of the paddle and they were clear.

Down below them they could see enormous sea anemones looking like hearth rugs that had been teased by a puppy. There were striped water snakes, bright blue starfish and large sea slugs. "*Bêche-de-mer*," said Paheero; "Chinaman he eat him mighty quick."

The canoe stopped over some black velvety-looking creatures. "You pick him up, Nelopee."

"Horrid," she said touching one, "slimy."

"You pick him up, you find big s'prise."

She dropped one into the canoe with a shudder, but in-

102

stead of a black jelly she saw before her a shell as round and white as a chicken's egg.

"He pull his coat inside him when you catch him; show you his white skin. Now you put him in water and he put on black coat again and walk away."

But the shock had been rather much for Mr. Cowrie, and he preferred to stay inside his house until the shadow overhead had floated by.

"You see that boy down there," said Paheero; "now you stay very quiet and I catch him for you."

So saying, he flipped it into the boat. Almost at once the creature began to swell, its eyes grew larger and bulged from its head, the parrot-like jaws opened and shut, and instead of being flat it was completely round.

"He'll burst," said Patrick, as the spines on its tummy stood erect from the tautness of its skin.

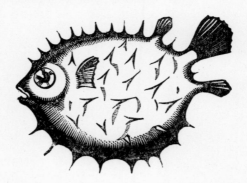

"You watch him," said Paheero; "he soon thin boy again." In a few minutes the fish had regained its normal figure, and when dropped into the water it lay on its back a few moments, then turned over, and swam to the bottom.

"Now I show you cow of the sea," said Paheero. "You sit very still and keep eye on clam shell down there.

"No!" he continued. "I think that cow shy, he stay in coral. We see 'nother 'fore long."

The canoe was drifting slowly with the current and the clean sandy bottom had given place to an accumulation of broken coral.

"Oh! You see that fellow there?" Paheero asked.

"Where?" asked Penelope.

"Where I poke."

"Can't see anything."

"Yes? No?"

"I can't."

"Oh, you blind, oh you dam' blind, you two boys. Now look—see!"

As Paheero dug at the bottom with his paddle, a lump of apparently dead coral floundered ahead.

"There he go, you see him now? There he go, now he lie pretend him dead stone—you step on him, you dead, no pretend. Yes, he got spikes all down back, one small spike in foot kill big man two minute. He real devvul, he hide in mud all covered lumps, bumps like stone—clam good boy, shark nice kind friend next him."

"We saw a huge shark over the other side," said Penelope.

"Plenty shark in deep water," said Paheero; "you keep

in shallow water when you swim, then you safe; but you mind where you step—don't put foot down, only on clean sand. See that little hole in rock?"

"Lots of them, little round ones, size of a shilling?"

"Yes, you step on them, you find small boy inside make hole in foot, plenty quick. He suck in anything come along near, then he chop off like sharp knife."

The rest of that evening and most of the next two days were occupied in making palm mats for the new roof. Paheero cut and split the fronds, and once the children got the hang of the plaiting all went along merrily. They told Paheero stories of London, of its underground trains, its electric signs and of the thousands of cars in the streets, none of which he believed.

"I think you been long enough on island begin tell lies like other white man," he said.

In return he told them stories of the Islands, of the fire-walking at Raiatea where they make a huge native oven perhaps twenty feet long and heat it up with sticks till the stones are white hot. Then the priests wave leaves of the sacred *ti* tree, and after that everybody walks about with bare feet on the hot stones and no one gets burnt.

"Unless he break *tabu*," said Paheero; "then he burn mighty bad. Yes! I see one fellow burn bad, him not stand on feet mighty long time."

"You saw it yourself?" asked Patrick.

"Yes, I see him. Priest say he break *tabu*, priest tell him not go. But he laugh and he go walk on stones. Then he fall down, mighty near die."

"Did you go?"

"Course I go, everyone go, white man go, white lady go."

"Wasn't it hot?"

105

"Hot in eyes, not hot on foot."

"Seems a blooming miracle," said Patrick.

"*Ti* leaves," said Paheero, "priests do mighty queer things along *ti* leaves."

He told them, too, of the old days and the big double war canoes capable of holding three hundred men, built with no other tools than a stone adze and a few sharpened bones.

"Can't see how they were built without tools," said Patrick.

"Stone adze," said Paheero, "chop very clean; shin bone sharpen up make good chisel."

"But how did they get the trees down?"

"Stone adze."

"And cut the planks?"

"Stone adze."

"Mighty rough, weren't they?"

"Coral along of sand, polish him quick," said Paheero.

Penelope was nearly sick when he told them how each new war canoe used to be launched over human bodies as rollers.

"What you making fuss about anyway?" he asked; "what you do in your island when one man kill 'nother man?"

"Hang him," said Patrick.

"Only bad men for sacrifice in Tahiti," said Paheero, "only thief, only man make murder. Chief say, 'When *pirogue* ready, fix eye along of him'. "

"Can't he escape?"

"He not know! He think all forgot. Then one day folk come along—say, 'Boy, you got fish hook you lend me?' When he look around find fish hook, club hit back of head, him finish."

But while these stories had been going on all three had been busy with the plaiting, and eventually the ground was strewn with mats, and the time came for fixing them to the bamboo rafters. Beginning at the eaves, they tied them each one a few inches above the one below, overlapping like tiles, until they reached the top.

The ridge itself required special treatment to prevent rain from getting through, and Paheero managed this by a double layer of mats bent over and secured with wooden pins.

He had hardly finished his last touches when the rain came down—not the soft drizzle one gets in England, but a downpour that sounded like gravel falling on a tin roof.

It was so thick that nothing could be seen beyond the reef. At times the rain blew along in sheets, making the water in the lagoon hiss and spit as if at the touch of hot metal. Lightning flashed and thunder rattled.

"I tell you yesterday it going to rain," said Paheero. "Good thing we hurry along finish roof."

"Can't we catch some for drinking?" asked Penelope.

"Plenty water in clam shells, two minutes' time."

"Clam shells?"

"Yes, big clams under pandanus, you not see? What you do with you eyes when you walk about?"

"Where are they?"

"Rain stop soon, then we go along. I show you. We find plenty water in shells, drink us mighty full."

The torrent ceased as suddenly as it had begun and the lagoon shone apple green as the purple clouds rolled out to sea. Then Paheero led them a race across the island.

They splashed through pools, they slipped on the soggy turf, and whenever they touched an overhanging branch they brought down cold showers on each other.

Patrick was the first to lift his head from the cool, fresh water that filled the clam shells lying about on the ground. He stopped drinking, not because he was satisfied, but because the trees were still dripping and the one over his particular shell was dispensing a very pretty trickle into the small of his back.

"I s'pose it's clean to drink?" he asked.

"Clean as the white of you eyeball," said Paheero. "I wash shells this morning when I see rain coming, all time you boys asleep. Treeko, you snore, and you wave hands 'bout you head, I think you have mighty queer dream."

"Thought I was in a canoe," said Patrick, "with some kind of a house on it, and it got upset and I was trying to turn it over."

"You dream of house on *pirogue*, that means you find turtle one day soon. Turtle, he swim like *pirogue* and all the time he carry own house on back. What happen when you try turn him over?"

"I woke up."

"And canoe?"

"Don't know, I think it sank."

"Then you lose your turtle, you not able turn him over, he get away sure thing."

"You don't believe that?" said Penelope.

108

"Course I believe that, and I tell you another sure thing. If you dream you go along road and you find big tree fall across road, too big walk over, an' you bend yourself, creep under branch, then one day you meet man bigger than youself and he make you go down on knee 'fore he let you pass."

"But if you can climb over?" asked Penelope.

"That mean you knock him down and you chief in his place," said Paheero. "Now we go along fetch kerosene tins, store water, then we fix bamboo rods along side of house. Tomorrow we make feast cel'brate finish house. Nelopee, I think we make dress for you in morning, then you proper native girl for feast."

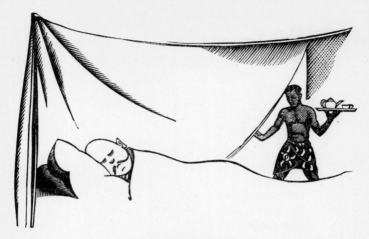

CHAPTER TEN

TIO AND FE'E

WHEN they woke next day Paheero had got a fire going and was boiling water in a couple of tins.

"You shut eyes little while longer," he said, "and I bring you tea like white lady gen'lman Rarotonga."

"Tea?" the children both asked in surprise.

"Yes, tea! All white person like tea, can't do one small thing any day 'fore he drink tea. You shut eyes now an' I bring you tea like you was gen'lman Rarotonga. When I lift *niau* leaf, that is you moskitto net. Now sar, you roll over and you open eyes little bit, then you shut 'em up quick, then you grunt, then you go sleep again. Now I make plenty noise, kick chair, bang table, then you turn over, grunt, say, what time? I say, s'ven dirty, sar. You say, s'ven dirty, can't you say save-an-thurrrty? I say, yes sar, s'ven dirty. Then you say, damfool; then you drink tea."

While this fun was going on Paheero had been soaking some leaves of the lime tree in the boiling water, and having added coconut milk he brought to each of the children a tin full. It was certainly not like any known blend of Indian or China tea, but it seemed to belong to the same family and they found it very refreshing.

"Now you want little bit bread made hot in front of fire, and little bit butter made cold on ice—then you wipe mouth, mess up nice clean cloth. Then you stretch you arms mighty big, say u-u-u-ugh; then you go fix on trousers, shirt, socks, shoes, ties, collars, belt, coat, and you hot an' sticky all whole rest of day."

"What about my skirt?" said Penelope.

"Yes! We fix you skirt today, just soon 's you finish tea, we go along fetch *purau* sticks. I kill little pig this morn, him all ready for feast. When we make quick work of dress we go on reef catch *tio*, that little oyster I show you other day. He have mighty sweet taste but he no good for pearl."

When the softened *purau* twigs had been washed clear of their muddy water, Paheero proceeded to beat them with a heavy stick to loosen the fibres. Then he collected the strands of inner bark and combed them through his fingers until they were smooth and pliable.

"Now Nelopee, you plait six cords make youself belt, then we fix fringe."

She did as he told her, and stretched the finished cord between two trees. Meanwhile Paheero continued his preparation of the fibre.

"Now you watch," he said, "I show you how make fringe. One piece *purau* bark, bend him in middle, once round this way, once round that way, pull through, pull tight, all finish. You do it! Mighty easy! That right, come

111

on, Treeko, now we all do him. When he long enough go round Nelopee, we each take fibre, tie him next fellow length of your finger down, that make skirt fit tight, mighty smart I think.

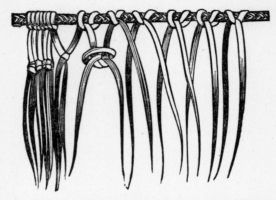

"Now, Nelopee, you come try see how he fit—yes, I think you mighty fine, you just like Tahiti dance girl."

"Wish you could see yourself," said Patrick.

"Wish I could too."

"You go look in pool under tree, you see yourself quick enough. Once on time no looking glass on islands; when girls want see themselves they look in dark pool, when they want pluck eyebrows they look in black coconut shell half full water."

"They didn't pluck their eyebrows in those days, did they?" asked Penelope.

"Girls always pluck brows, same thing men always shave chin."

"How could they shave without razors?"

"Shark's tooth mighty good, or p'raps scale from big fish."

112

"It sounds awful," said Patrick.

"Say, Nelopee! Don't you go in water with dress, him spoil in salt water—I tell you funny story happen along Marquesas Islands.

"One day, long time ago, mishnary ship sails in Nuka-Hiva harbour. All boys on island very glad go in *pirogues* visit ship. All girls very sad 'cause chief he say *tabu*, no *vahine* in *pirogues*; if girls want see ship then he say they swim. Girls say if we go in water our tapa cloth all fall in little bits. Chief say, plenty fine trees on island, if you want go in water you make dress nice green leaves. Then all girls make dress big green leaves, an' each one she swim out to ship. When mishnary see girls come board ship, no clothes on topsides, he frown very much. While he go inside ship look for dress, goats on ship see nice green leaves make skirt of girls; goats hungry, they no seen any green thing many weeks; they make run at girls, eat up all dress. When mishnary come back he find girls no clothes anywhere, all eaten up by goats. Then he very scandalize, give each one new dress from white lady Londoni."

While they were talking they had wandered towards the canoe. "I think I go make fire in *umu*, and you boys go find oysters," said Paheero. "You take *pirogue*, go close along shore where I show you other day, bring back all shell you able. Treeko, you take spear see if you more clever catch fish than you was."

He pushed them off in the canoe and turned inland to collect firewood. Penelope took the paddle while Patrick stood ready with the spear.

"Mind where you're going," said Patrick; "there's coral ahead."

"You sit down or we'll upset," she rejoined.

"Where did he say those oysters were?"

"Somewhere along by the pandanus—wasn't that an awful story about the war canoes?"

"Doesn't much matter if they were dead."

"He said there used to be crowds of sacrifices."

"Only of criminals, and they didn't eat them anyway."

"They used to eat their enemies in war time," persisted Penelope.

"For heaven's sake look where you're goin'," said Patrick, as the canoe grated on some coral and then floated clear again.

"Are *you* watching for fish?"

"There aren't any, you're frightening them with your paddling. Keep out to the right—that's better—now in again, now straight on. Let her drift, there's a breeze. We're nearly past the point."

Then they realized they had gone too far for the oysters.

"Never mind," said Patrick, "I hate them anyway. Let's go round the point."

"Can you see anything?"

"Not yet. Half a mo'—go on, give a couple of strokes— why, it's the blooming old bird nesting place—whoop, there they go."

The birds rose, but settled again.

"Those are the bushes round the *marae*."

"Let her float," said Patrick. "Sh-h-h, don't speak," he whispered, "there's something moving."

"Where? Can't see it."

"Talk low! On the right of the bushes. It's Paheero, sh-h, he's kneeling down."

"What's he doing?"

"Can't see. Lifting something up and down—now he's burying it in the sand."

114

"Come on, let's get back; he'd be awfully annoyed if he saw us. It's probably his religion, one of those little 'tikis' he told us about, little images they take about and worship."

"Go on, then, get the canoe round," said Patrick. "Look the other way and pretend we haven't seen him."

They paddled back against the wind, trying to appear as if they had seen nothing.

"What about those oysters?" Penelope asked.

"Oh, never mind them, we'll say we couldn't find any."

As they headed across the lagoon they could see that whatever else Paheero had been doing, he had at any rate got a fire going, and this reminded them that they were supposed to be fishing. Patrick stood up to get a better view of the channel. BUMP! The canoe hit a submerged rock and Patrick took a header into the water. Penelope's raucous laughter might have been heard in Tahiti.

"I knew you'd do it," he spluttered when he came to the surface.

"How could I see with you in the way?" she asked, still guffawing.

"Well, keep her steady till I get in."

Next moment the whole caboodle turned over. Penelope was in the water beside him, and the out-rigger, having made a half circle in the air, just missed their heads.

"I knew *you'd* do that," spluttered Penelope.

"Well, why didn't you say so?"

"You should have got in at the end."

"What's the good of telling me that now?"

"Come on, let's get her over."

The canoe was lying bottom up and the problem of righting her was not an easy one. Each time they got her half-way, the weight of the outrigger pulled her back again. Eventually they clambered on to some coral and succeeded in toppling her over.

"How are we going to bail her?" asked Patrick.

"Blowed if I know."

"Swim ashore and get a coconut shell."

"You go—you upset her."

"You upset me first."

"You go on. I'll sit here and hold her."

"Well, don't sit on a clam shell," said Patrick, as he headed for the shore.

"Allo, Treeko, you find plenty oysters?" asked Paheero, who was now chopping wood.

"I want a coconut shell or an old tin," said Patrick.

"What for you want that?"

"To bail the canoe. We upset her."

"Oh Gloria looja! Where you do that?"

"Near the pass in the reef."

"Where's Nelopee?"

"With the canoe."

"Come on, I come with you; you not want coconut, I show you how fix him quick."

On reaching the canoe, Paheero took hold of one end and pulled it sharply towards him. Immediately a spurt of water shot over the other end. Then he pushed it away, and water splashed over him. Each quick jerk threw out more, and in a few moments it was empty.

"Where's paddle and spear?" asked Paheero.

"The spear sank, and—"

At this moment Penelope gave a wild shriek. "There's something on my leg," she called, "come quickly, I can't move—quickly, quickly," she screamed, "it's got my other foot—I can't move!"

Paheero was by her side in an instant. "Where's spear?"

"It sank."

"Wher'bouts?"

"There!"

"Don't move, don't try move one inch."

Then he plunged into the water. A second later he was beside her with the spear. "Don't you move one inch, keep you foot still—agh!"

Penelope shrieked and clutched Paheero. The water seemed filled with ink. They could see nothing below the surface.

He had driven the spear into something close beside her and now he held it pressed firmly into the coral.

"It's tearing my skin," she cried.

"Bring *pirogue*," he called to Patrick, who meantime had retrieved the paddle.

"Now, Nelopee, you hold tight on canoe, leave you legs in water. That boy nearly dead, him very small *fe'e*, we soon fix him."

The water was clearing and Paheero went below to investigate. The top of his spear moved up and down as if jabbing at something, Penelope screamed again. A moment later Paheero returned to the surface, smiling.

"Only very small boy," he said; "he dead two seconds."

Penelope lay across the canoe trying to lift her feet.

Suddenly they came up with such speed that she nearly went over the other side. Her legs waved in the air—and clinging to them were the arms of an octopus.

Paheero, swimming close beside, removed the spear from its body, and one by one he pulled the tentacles from her legs. Where each had been there was an ugly line of red weals showing where the numerous suckers had gripped her skin.

"Can't we throw it overboard?" said Patrick, shuddering, as he surveyed the speckled body still writhing in the canoe.

"No, don't you throw him nowhere," said Paheero. "We eat him with small pig. Him very sweet."

"I'd rather starve," said Penelope.

When they reached the shore Paheero fetched some rain water and bathed her scars, then he rubbed in the oil taken from the crab, and finally he bound up her legs in bandages of cool leaves.

"Now you come along sit down in new house while we boys fix *umu*, then one time soon we have big feed."

He fetched her an armful of grass to lie on and then joined Patrick at the oven.

"I think Nelopee mighty dam' lucky she caught by little *fe'e*. If him big fellow she not get away for long while, p'raps not ever. *Fe'e* hold on long time, then she fall, then he catch head; then she drown."

"I've never seen such a filthy looking creature," said Patrick.

"Yes, him mighty wicked, him son of Tumu, mighty great octopus, way back many time afore world begin. His arms so big strong, he hold sky down on earth, not let any small piece o' light come in. All world dark, black dark. Then one day big god belong fruit, he come along say fruit

118

no grow in dark, trees no grow in dark, nothin' grow in dark 'cept big octopus. Then he kill big octopus and sky jump mighty high, and light fall on world. Then trees begin grow, fish begin grow, flowers an' crabs, and coral begin grow in lagoon an'—but now I think *umu* ready."

Paheero interrupted his story to scrape away the wood ash from the hot stones in the oven, and to lay in place the little pig he had prepared for cooking along with the taro and bananas. He covered them all up, and continued his story of the creation.

"What like you think first man? You not know? I tell you—just one big jellyfish, no arms, no legs, no anything. Then Tane, him god of Beauty, him father of all little gods, him pick white coral and make bones for man, then he pick bark from trees and he make skin for him, then he take coconut fibre and he make hair for him. Then man stand up on legs, but he like tree, not see, not smell. Then Tane make holes in head for ears and he speak in them, then he make nose and mouth and blow in them, then he make eyes. Then first fellow open eyes and make mighty big blow through mouth and, when he blow, it make whistle; and ever and ever, very long time, whistle *tabu* 'cept for chief."

When they went to see how Penelope was getting on, she was asleep, so they wandered along to the surviving log of the fallen palm.

"We make mighty fine *pirogue*," said Paheero, picking up the adze and sending chips flying in all directions. "You go along fetch burnt sticks from fire, then we draw lines on log where we work."

Patrick went off, to find that Penelope had waked up and had gone to wait for them by the oven.

"Hullo, how're the legs?" he asked.

119

"Fine. When's food?"

"Don't know, in about half an hour I expect. Paheero's making a canoe."

After her sleep Penelope seemed entirely recovered. There was scarcely a mark on her leg, and the new fibre skirt which she was wearing swung like a kilt as she followed Patrick to the scene of operations.

"Allo! Allo, Nelopee! Ah, you not Nelopee no longer, now you Tuamotu girl in Tuamotu dress. I think I call you Tiare cause you skin white like Tiare flower. How you legs, Tiare?"

"Fine, thanks. Hardly a mark."

"That 'cause of oil, oil mighty good on skin. One day we make copra oil, rub in skin, make skin soft, keep salt water out when you swim long time. Got that wood, Treeko? Good boy, I just finish make topsides flat, then we draw line all way round. This end *mua*, how you call bow; other end *muri*, stern. Now we make line both sides same thing. White man always have measure sticks, native man he use eye. Why for you got two eyes if you not use them both side?"

"I'm starving," said Penelope.

"Oho! You want *kai-kai*, you always got empty basket ready for *kai-kai*. You go along open *umu*, find *puaka*. Treeko he help me turn *pirogue*, then we come along double quick."

Penelope trotted off.

"Yes, Treeko boy, I tell you oil mighty good for sick skin, and Treeko, I tell you one thing you never tell anyone no time ever. Treeko, if you want pinch thing belong other fellow, then you take off all you dress, put lots of oil all over you body. If other fellow wake up try catch you, his hands slip on you body, then you get away quick, he no

120

find you. If you go night time and you rub black ash on you face, then other fellow not know who he see."

After this bit of advice they started off together, but Paheero said that he had forgotten his adze and must return for it. Meanwhile Patrick joined Penelope, and they both sat waiting.

CHAPTER ELEVEN
PEARLS

"I VOTE we begin," said Penelope, after they had waited what seemed a very long time.

"Hadn't I better go and look for him?" suggested Patrick. "He's probably back at the *marae*."

"Listen!" said Penelope.

They could hear some disturbance in the undergrowth. Next minute Paheero lurched through the trees and flopped down beside them.

"My head go round and round," he said; "think sun hit him when I make *pirogue*, think I grow like white man, weak in head."

He refused to eat anything. "Don't want you boys following me round island," he said, "don't want no one messin' about. My head sick. When my head sick I stay by self."

"We weren't following you," said Patrick.

122

"You stay along this side of island—what for you come messin' about in *pirogue*? You stay along here."

No, he didn't want any food, they could eat it themselves; he was going to sleep.

Next morning he was still huddled up where they had left him. "My head full of coral," he said, "big lumps. When I move he go bump bump." He refused to touch anything they offered him, but just before midday he got up and wandered off alone. "You boys stay here, cook you own food, then you go along canoe see fish for silly dam' uncle."

By the evening, however, he had quite recovered. He was in fact extraordinarily cheerful, told them how glad he was they had come to his island, and that they must stay with him always. One day soon they'd go pearl fishing, find big pearls, these he'd go and sell at Marama and bring back lots of food. Yes, he knew where to find the big blue-lipped shells, the ones that had the largest pearls.

Why hadn't he got them before? the children asked.

Oh, it was difficult by himself; but now he had someone to manage the canoe it was easy. No, he didn't care if the *rahui* was on or off. What business had the French Government making laws in the Tuamotus? Pearls belonged to him in his own island, he'd go fetch them just whenever he liked.

When would he go?

Why, he'd go the very next day, they'd all go first thing in the morning. "Where you put rope?" he asked.

"In the old hut," said Penelope.

"We put him in *pirogue* an' we tie on lump o' coral for anchor and we put in knife an' spear, and I bring along new rope and we have piece wood make float, then we ready."

123

Next morning while the tide was still ebbing, and before the first signs of dawn, they were awakened by Paheero, who announced that food was ready. Much to their surprise they found half a dozen hen's eggs ready boiled, and he had also made another infusion of lime tea.

"When stones bang in head yesterday I lie down along of pandanus, get mighty big fright; chicken he jump up under my leg screech screech screech, my st mach hop mighty bad. I think where he hide himself on island, p'raps he hide eggs too. Yes! He have seven eggs, I leave him one so he find place again."

"How do we eat them?" asked Patrick.

"With you teeth, with you fingers; they boil in water long while."

Breakfast finished, they pushed off in the canoe and followed the line of the coast to the west. Once round the point they headed for the centre of the lagoon. Paheero had on his forehead a pair of diving goggles, held round his head by a strip of rubber. They were made of two circles of wood, rather like napkin rings, into which pieces of glass had been fitted.

"You promised us any pearls we find," said Penelope.

"That's right, you have all pearls *you* find—but I don't think we get very rich today, I think wind blow strong one time soon."

They continued their course for a mile or more.

"Now, Treeko, you take paddle, keep her go slow; when I call, then you stop."

He knelt down in the canoe, peering into the water.

It was gradually getting shallower, and Penelope could see the blurred forms of the coral some thirty or forty feet below.

"Very slow," said Paheero, "very slow now—little bit

124

more, *now* we stop. I think that nice piece of coral just behind."

He had already tied the two ropes together, and now he dropped the stone overboard. Then he paddled backwards, paying out the rope as he went along. "When I come up top each time you pull in little bit rope, then we always look new piece o' ground."

He pulled the goggles over his eyes, swung his legs over the side, muttered something to himself, and began to breathe deeply. For a minute or more he sat there taking in huge breaths, then without a word he dropped overboard. He shot down some twelve or twenty feet before turning over to continue the journey head first to the bottom.

They could just see him groping about below, but the water was too deep to make out much of what he was doing.

"He's down ages," said Penelope.

"Five minutes?"

"More like ten."

"He couldn't be as long as that."

They both peered into the water.

"Can you see him?" asked Penelope.

"Not a sign."

A thud in the canoe made them both sit up. Paheero was hanging on the gunwale behind them, panting. In the bottom of the canoe was an oyster shell about seven inches across.

"Leave rope where he is," he said at last; "I think this good spot."

He breathed deeply for a few minutes and then again he dropped out of sight.

"Let's count," said Patrick.

They had only reached sixty-two when he arrived with another shell.

"I thought it was ten times longer," said Patrick.

"Pull rope little bit," said Paheero.

Again and again he went down, at intervals of five or six minutes. When they did not count he seemed to be away for hours, but when they kept time it was never more than sixty or seventy seconds.

After half-an-hour he climbed into the canoe to rest.

"I think we come back tomorrow with basket. I take him down fill him quick."

"Can we open these?" asked Patrick.

"Yes, we open quick enough," said Paheero, taking the knife. Then he forced it between the two sides of the shell and, pressing downwards, cut through the big muscle that held them together.

"Now you look for pearl," he said; "p'raps you find him in flesh, p'raps you find him in shell."

They searched through the slimy "mantle" and ran their fingers over the inside of the shell, but not as much as a pin head showed up.

Penelope was about to throw the inside overboard when Paheero stopped her. "Not now, not now!" he said. "You throw in now an' we have all sharks in lagoon round here two minutes. When we finish, then we throw him over."

"Can't *we* dive anywhere?" asked Penelope. "Is it all as deep as this?"

"Yes, plenty places where you dive, but not where you get big shell. Big pearl only in big shell. I take you, now, where p'raps you find little pearl. This mighty good spot for big shell, I come back here tomorrow with basket."

Leaving the anchor with its buoy to mark the place where they had been diving, they headed the canoe across the lagoon towards the eastern reef. After a time the water became shallow and the sand and coral below them became as clear as in a rock pool.

"Now, Nelopee," said Paheero, "you put goggles over your eyes and you hop over, see what you find. That's right: you sit one side little while, say prayer, take big breath. Don't you fetch up anything smaller 'n six inches, or French Gov'nment fine you thousand francs."

Penelope took a deep breath, held her nose and let go of the canoe. Down, down she went, with her face screwed up tight, till her feet touched bottom. Then she opened her eyes and it seemed to her like being inside a big green bottle. But it was almost impossible to keep her balance and her feet had already left the ground when she grabbed at a rock to steady herself. There wasn't a sight or sign of an oyster, and, as she peered about, there were strange shapes and shadows, and she seemed to sense large eyes blinking at her from holes in the coral. Her hand touched something slimy. She stubbed her toe on something sharp.

It was no good, she had had enough. She struck out with her arms and began to move slowly towards the surface. What a long way it was! Would she ever get there before she burst? This beastly green water in every direction and light overhead. Pouf! Her head popped out of the water and she clutched at the gunwale. She was unable to speak as she hung on, breathless.

127

"How many shell you fetch?" asked Paheero, smiling.

"Couldn't see a thing," said Penelope. "Nothing but coral and loathsome things growing everywhere."

"Can I go?" asked Patrick, eagerly.

"Yes, you go now. Don't forget little prayer, all divers say little prayer."

Splash! In went Patrick.

It was a long swim to the bottom, and when he got there he could see no more than Penelope had seen. As he groped along the bottom, a large fish dashed from behind a boulder, almost hitting him in the face. Finally, he put his feet on the sand, gave a good kick and came to the surface very much quicker than he had gone down.

"How many you bring back?" asked Paheero. "Same as Nelopee, I guess. I think *pirogue* sink if you fill her too quick!"

"There aren't any there," said Patrick.

"Not any there?" laughed Paheero. "Not any there? I see plenty there right now?"

"Where?" asked the children.

"Why, all over the place where you been."

"You can see them from here?" asked Patrick, still puffing.

"Yes, I see them, lots of them."

"I don't believe it!" said Penelope.

Paheero took the goggles from Patrick: "I show you," he said. Slipping into the water, he swam below, wrenching at the rocks, now here, now there. In a few moments he was back with four shells, two in each hand.

"Place full of shell," he said. "But they small, they too small."

"Well, why couldn't *we* see them?"

"'Cause you not got pearl eyes," said Paheero. "All folk same thing first time, see nothing. When you been dive many times, you get pearl eyes, see shell hid away in rock like land crab in hole. P'raps if very smart you find shell in holes with you hand."

"Not me," said Penelope.

"I think you right, p'raps Koiru catch you. Yes, eel, him mighty big, him long as you. When he small he go in hole, then he sit down grow big. Then he grow

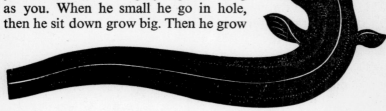

too big come out. He stay there all time."

"How does he live, then?" asked Penelope.

"Just sit still do nothing, keep mouth open all day, like folk in Papeete. When little fish swim along, not see big open mouth, then he snap quick. That finish little fish."

"Would they bite us?"

"Huh! Would they bite? If they bite, all mighty well, p'raps you lose just one finger. When Koiru bite, he just shut mouth and hold on tight till you drown. Then you make *kai-kai* for lots of queer things."

Paheero had been hanging leisurely on to the outrigger. Suddenly he gripped the canoe and swung himself in.

129   E*

"*Ma-o!*" he said.

"Gosh!" cried Patrick. "Sharks! Look at them!"

A dozen fins were cutting the water.

"Those boys come just few minutes late for dinner. How you like meet them when you down below? Huh! Those fellows, when they come all together, they attack mighty quick. Give me paddle. I think we find enough shell today."

As the canoe moved homewards it was followed by a shoal of small sharks.

"If we threw in the oysters now, wouldn't it distract them?" asked Penelope.

"No fear, you throw nothing nowhere," said Paheero. "You get throwing things about, we have big fellows come along, then p'raps we have trouble."

"Lucky they didn't come ten minutes sooner," said Patrick.

"That 'cause you say prayer. If you forget say prayer, one of you not go home along of me, sure thing."

"I'm *never* going in again," said Patrick.

"Nor me," said Penelope.

"You forget all 'bout that tomorrow when we go along find big shell," said Paheero. "There they go," he added, as the sharks turned about and left them. "All gone away back in shallow water. These small boys not like deep water; p'raps something bit bigger come along finish them."

"We've never opened the small shell," said Penelope, as they unloaded the canoe.

"Well, you take knife, see what you find. Mind fingers, don't hold him in hand, put him on *pirogue*. That's right."

"Nothing in it," said Penelope.

"No, I think you not find very great many. Squeeze him tight in fingers, p'raps you miss little one."

130

"Nothing in this either," said Penelope.

"Nor this," said Patrick.

"You not using fingers," said Paheero, "you must pull him through fingers same as me."

"It's worse than cleaning chickens," said Penelope.

"Say! Look what you leave behind you," exclaimed Paheero. "Here's pearl!"

"A real one?" asked Penelope, excitedly.

"Course it's real," said Patrick. "What you expect to find, Woolworth necklace?"

"Is it valuable?" asked Penelope.

"Ten francs, perhaps. He mighty small, colour bad."

"Is that all, really?"

" Yes, he little seed pearl, make brooch along of others."

"Any chance of finding more?"

"P'raps you do—plenty small pearl in small shell."

But they didn't find any more and, that excitement being over, they were very ready for some food.

"*Pisupo*," said Paheero, "we have *kai-kai pisupo*." This time it was baked beans and pork that came out of the tin.

"I'm glad we got one pearl at any rate," said Penelope.

"Tomorrow we get plenty big shell," said Paheero.

Next morning they were on the lagoon at the same early hour and, having found the buoy that they had left to mark the spot, Paheero got ready to dive. He had spent some time the evening before in making a net bag, and plaiting long strips of *purau* bark into a three-ply rope. Weighting the bag with a stone, he now lowered it over the side before going down himself.

He was away for little more than a minute, and his return to the surface was the signal to haul up the bag. In it were seven shells. Each subsequent dive was also successful. Sometimes it was two or three very large shells, perhaps ten inches across; at others it might be six or more of a smaller size.

"Take five years grow good shell," said Paheero. "You leave him one year more, then he worth twice the money."

They were working over a deep pocket in the coral, and Paheero spent more and more time under water.

After one of these longer dives he seemed particularly exhausted, and when he threw his head back to breathe, a few drops of blood trickled from his nose.

"I think *pirogue* full 'nough for you boys paddle home," he said, "p'raps I done enough today."

It was no joke paddling the heavy canoe against the wind, but Patrick and Penelope took it in turns and eventually they reached home.

Paheero treated the matter very lightly. "Nothin' to make fuss about," he said, "just stay down a bit long. Few years ago I dive hundred and fifty feet, stay down three minutes. Now I go hundred feet, stay two minutes only, and nose bleed. Not very good, p'raps I get old."

He opened the shells as they went along, but only one pearl was found, and that a small one.

"I put him safe in house," said Paheero. "One day we find fellow much bigger."

CHAPTER TWELVE
A RUM IDEA

"I CAN'T make it out," said Penelope, a few days later. "Paheero seems to have changed. He doesn't seem to want us near him, especially in the evenings, and he doesn't answer when I speak to him. He chops away at his new canoe and hardly says a word. Why was he up here by himself before we came?" she asked.

"Might be getting away from the police," suggested Patrick.

"I'm scared of him every time I see him with that knife in his hands."

Patrick didn't say anything to this. He, too, had felt a bit scared, once or twice, when he thought he'd seen a funny look in Paheero's eye.

"I wish to goodness we could get down to the other islands and p'raps find Uncle," he said.

"Can't we borrow the old canoe?" suggested Penelope.

"Don't know. He says he wants to make copra."

"I wish he wasn't so moody—one minute he's cross, next minute he's laughing."

"Where is he now?" asked Patrick.

"At his canoe."

"Let's go and get fresh grass for the hut," said Penelope.

At the far side of the island they found Paheero, sitting on the ground with an empty bottle beside him. To their surprise, he greeted them with tremendous delight.

"Ah, you boys, you just come nice time, just very nice right time carry my pore legs back along house. When I bend down, lumps o' coral fall out of head into feet; now head very light, feet very heavy."

He tried to get up but collapsed on to the ground.

"I think I put *kai-kai* in my pore sad belly," he went on, "then he stay more steady. Now he wobble just like water in *pirogue*. How many fish you catch, Treeko? Nelopee, you put plenty fish soak in limes? Good boys, you two good boys. Say! Where's that fish?" he said as he struggled to his feet and stumbled towards the house.

It was lucky for the children that they had put plenty of fish to "cook" for, no sooner had they reached the house than, without hesitation or delay, Paheero plunged his fingers into the lime juice and began eating the fish as fast as he could. He paid no attention to the children. The amount he ate would have been enough for three ordinary appetites. He swallowed every scrap he could see, and when he had laid hands on the last particle of fish, he got up and floundered off through the trees without another word.

"He's mad," said Patrick.

"Drunk," said Penelope.

"Where did he get that bottle?" asked Patrick.

"Had it buried, I suppose."

134

"That's what he brought back with him in those cases," said Patrick, "and that's what he was digging up the other day when we saw him on the other side of the point."

"Bet you he's gone for more now," said Penelope.

"I wish *we* could get away," said Patrick, with emphasis.

"We'll have to if he gets worse."

"How will we go? In the canoe?"

"Yes, in the canoe! Come on, let's try to get it now," said Penelope eagerly.

A few minutes later they heard Paheero calling to them: "What you boys doing with canoe?"

"Fishing," said Patrick.

"What for you want fish? You bellies full!"

"It's for tomorrow," said Penelope, not liking to add that it was he who had eaten everything there was to eat and that they were still hungry.

Paheero's only answer to this was a grunt. Then, after a pause, he called, "You come look see what I find."

"What is it?" asked Penelope, as they reached where he was sitting.

"Rum, good rum! I bring him back Marama. I bring back three box full rum, and I bury in sand. I tell you why I hide bottle in sand, 'cause I think Treeko bad boy. I think Treeko real bad boy. If he see bottle, he drink, then he drunk, then he have lumps of coral in head like Hiro— no, not Hiro, Paheero, I mean. Why for I say Hiro? Hiro, him god of thief. One time Rarotonga they call ME Hiro —yes, white man call ME Hiro. I tell you 'bout that other time, not now. Treeko, you go fetch coconut shell, then we all drink rum like white man."

"I don't want any," said Patrick.

"Nor me," said Penelope. "I don't like it."

135

"Not like, not like, you not like rum? O' course you like rum. Treeko, you go fetch nuts."

There was nothing for it but to do as he was told.

"I tell you what I think, Nelopee," whispered Paheero, drawing unpleasantly close, "I think I have fight with Treeko. When I have rum, then I like fight. What you think? P'raps I kill Treeko. Big cut in head, like old bone you see in bush." Paheero laughed a horrible, drunken chuckle.

Penelope was aghast. Paheero's drooping eye was almost shut, his mouth hung open and dribbled. He knocked the neck off another bottle and poured the raw liquid into his mouth. His hand shook and he spilled it over his bare chest.

"You open you mouth and have some," he said.

"No, I hate it."

"I say, you have some."

"Please, no!"

"I tell you, you open you mouth," he said, moving to get up.

"No!" shrieked Penelope, "I can't bear it."

Patrick arrived at this moment. "Can't find shells," he said.

"Can't find shells, can't find shells? You drunk, Treeko. Can't find shells! *I* go find shells. Treeko drunk, poor Treeko, he can't find shells."

He put the bottle down and made an effort to rise, but his knees gave way under him and he lay on the ground laughing.

"My legs like jellyfish," he gasped. "My legs like jelly-fish, all wobble. Nelopee, where you go? Nelopee, you give me bottle, come sit down."

136

She handed him the bottle. "I think I'll go and help Treeko find the coconuts," she said.

He tried to pour some more liquid into his mouth. "Good girl Nelopee, you help Treeko find nuts. I think—yes—I think I go—sleep. You—help Treeko—nuts . . . "

His head drooped and he fell forward insensible.

Instead of looking for the coconut shells, which in reality were lying all about the place, Patrick had been collecting oddments from Paheero's hut and carrying them to the shore.

Now was their chance for the getaway, and in less than

five minutes the canoe was afloat and they were straining every muscle to increase their distance from the shore.

Every few minutes they glanced back, in dread that Paheero had discovered their flight and might in some fiendish way be following them. But there was no sign of him. It was a long while before they dared to relax their efforts. At last, however, they decided to have a breather.

"What are we going to do now?" asked Patrick.

"Don't know. Let's go on, anywhere, away. Where's Marama?"

"Somewhere down there, I s'pose, it must be inside the lagoon."

"Keep on paddling," said Penelope.

Patrick put in another hard spell with the paddle. "Phew!" he said, "I'm blown."

"Give me the paddle, then," said Penelope. "I wish I'd been wearing the *pareu*—we might have sailed, the wind's after us."

"The *pareu's* in the bow under the bananas," said Patrick, "I thought it might come in handy; and there's some water and a couple of tins of beef. That's all we've got."

"You're sure he can't follow?" asked Penelope, looking behind her anxiously.

"No fear, he was only burning out the centre of his new canoe yesterday. He hadn't even found an outrigger."

"I feel absolutely sick," said Penelope. "Didn't think he could be so loathsome."

"He's all right when he's sober," said Patrick.

"You know what he was going to do with you?" Penelope asked.

"No, what?"

"Murder you," said Penelope.

"ME?" said Patrick, astonished.

"Yes," said Penelope. "Hit you on the head, he said, like the skull in the bush."

"Golly! Are you *sure* he isn't following us?"

"Let's get that *pareu* up as a sail," said Penelope. "Fix it to the paddle."

"And the spear," agreed Patrick. "I'm glad I pinched that."

"I think he's worse than the octopus," said Penelope, shuddering.

"No wonder he didn't want us messing about, as he called it, at the *marae*, when he had all those bottles hidden there," said Patrick, thoughtfully.

They fastened one end of the *pareu* to the spear and the other end to the paddle and, holding up the brightly coloured length of cotton as a sail, they were soon bowling along before the wind.

CHAPTER THIRTEEN

PENELOPE GROWS WINGS

"TREES ahead," announced Penelope.

"It'll be dark before we get there," said Patrick.

"D'you think we can land in the dark?"

"We'll have to: we can't stay out all night in this."

"Hope to goodness the natives are friendly."

"Hope to goodness they haven't got any rum."

"What'll we tell them?" asked Penelope, as they drew nearer to the shore.

"Say we're looking for Uncle."

"What about Paheero?"

"Say he lent us the canoe."

"Can't see any fires," Penelope said presently. "I 'spect they're all asleep—only hope we don't scare 'em."

The canoe bumped and scrunched, then floated on.

"Shallow water again."

"Sh-h-h, they'll hear us."

Very gently they moved towards the land. It was inky dark, but their eyes could just distinguish the line of the shore.

"Let's sleep near the canoe," whispered Penelope as they ran aground on a sandy beach.

"Give a hand and we'll haul it up," said Patrick.

An hour later Patrick was awakened by Penelope's screams.

"Let go!" she cried. "Let go! I can't bear it! I don't want it—take it away!"

The moon had risen, and Patrick could see her sitting up and waving her arms.

"Who is it?" asked Patrick. "Where is he? I can't see anyone."

"Where are we?" Penelope said, rubbing her eyes.

"We're on Marama, who's troubling you?"

"Where's Paheero?" she asked.

"Miles away."

"Sure?"

"Dead sure."

"Must have been dreaming, I thought he was making me drink rum."

"For goodness' sake, don't shout. You scared the life out of me."

"Did I talk?" she asked.

"No, you yelled. If you do it again we'll have all the natives on top of us."

"Sorry. Let's go to sleep again."

But it was difficult to settle down, and the first light of day found Patrick on hands and knees peering through the undergrowth.

Penelope crept after him.

"See anything?" she asked.

"Nothing!"

"Where are they?"

"Can't see anybody. Why, the island is tiny," he said, standing up. "P'raps it's not Marama at all."

At that moment a dead palm frond came swishing down from a tree just behind them.

Patrick dropped to his knees.

"Phew! Made me jump," he said.

"Made you drop," said Penelope.

"I don't believe there's anyone here at all," said Patrick.

141

"I'm sure there's not."

"Perhaps there are people living over there," he said, pointing across the half mile of water that separated them from the next island.

There seemed to be a whole chain of islets. Most of them were small, but there was a big one at the end. Was that Marama, they wondered.

Penelope began to feel hungry. Patrick did, too, when the idea was put to him; so, opening one of the tins with the spear they sat down to a breakfast of corned beef and bananas.

Except for some scrubby undergrowth and the palms, there was nothing of interest on the little island, and after their meal they pushed off in the canoe and made for the next one.

It was bigger, and here there were definite signs of humanity. Coconuts, chopped open, lay spread on the ground; others, tied in hanks, were suspended from poles. Several trestles, like Paheero's, held trays of drying copra.

"Filthy—smell it," said Penelope, wrinkling up her nose.

"This is better," said Patrick, pointing to a large wooden trough filled with flowers soaking in oil.

"It's like scent," said Penelope, sniffing.

"It probably *is* scent."

"Bet it's that oil they sell in Tahiti. I don't believe there's anyone on this island either," Penelope added, looking around.

"There must be," said Patrick. "They're probably hiding and watching us."

"Let's walk round. Why, there isn't even a hut; it can't be deserted?"

"Well, it looks like it."

142

"P'raps an enemy tribe has raided them. But I don't see any blood about the place."

"They probably come over from some other island to work here," said Patrick, "to make copra and this scent stuff."

"Of course, why didn't we think of that before? Come on, let's shift, it's no good staying here. P'raps we shall meet them on the way over."

So they set off once more in their canoe to cover the mile of water that lay between them and the next island, an island which rose rather higher out of the lagoon and was covered with luxuriant foliage.

"MacCarthy is supposed to be down here," said Patrick.

"So are we," said Penelope.

"I wonder if Uncle has got back," said Patrick. "Bet he'll be surprised to see us! If he's not here we'll get in a schooner and go to Hikueru. I do wish we'd escaped from Paheero before."

"We'd never have managed it; Paheero wasn't drunk enough, he'd have swum after us."

"He was bad enough one or two nights. D'you remember after he'd been telling us about the white men who used to take pot shots at the natives from passing schooners? He went off and didn't come back again the whole evening."

"I don't believe that yarn anyway."

"He swears it's true. He says his grandfather was killed like that."

"And do you believe what he called 'black-birding'?" Penelope asked.

"Enticing the natives on board a schooner and then sailing away with them and making them slaves? He said that's why they hated the white man and killed him whenever they got the chance."

143

"I don't blame them," said Penelope. "But I wish some-one had kidnapped *him*."

"What's that in the water?" she said a few minutes later as they went along.

"Where?"

"On your left, just behind you."

Patrick was sitting in the bow working the paddle over the right gunwale. He turned, to see a large shark close beside him.

"It's all right," he said, "he can't harm us in the canoe."

"He's awfully big."

"Not very."

"He's as long as the canoe," said Penelope.

"Gosh, so he is!"

"Keep paddling, he may go away."

A bump on the bottom of the boat scared them both.

"He went underneath—he's here on the right," said Patrick. "Did you see that?" he added "He snapped at the paddle."

"P'raps he's playing," said Penelope, trying to appear brave.

"He's at it again. Can't you heave something at him?"

"There's one tin of beef."

"Sling it hard," said Patrick. "Wait till he's near the surface, don't miss him. Heavens! Sit still. Gosh! I thought you'd upset us."

144

"I hit him," said Penelope.

"Good shot! He's gone. No, he isn't, he's back again."

"Paddle hard, we're half-way there."

"Can't work harder, I'm blown."

"Give me the paddle."

He turned to pass it back to her, but as he did so a vicious snap twitched it out of his hands into the water.

This was awful; they were still half a mile from land and, now that they were no longer moving, the brute swam round and round them in circles, sometimes diving under and scraping the bottom of the canoe, sometimes coming close alongside and turning over to show a glimpse of its white belly.

They shivered as they sat there helpless and almost speechless with fear.

"Can't we use the spear?" said Penelope.

"We'd never get him, and it's too weak anyway."

"Try!"

A vicious bump on the side nearly upset them.

Now the shark was getting more brazen. It hit the canoe with its head, it lashed water over it with its tail, and the only weapon they had was the spear, the light spear that had been made for parrot fish.

"Try and get his eye," said Penelope.

Patrick tried, but at that moment the shark turned over and the spear skidded along its skin, sticking in one of the gills. Patrick gave an extra push. Next moment they were nearly upset by a smashing blow from the tail.

Penelope noticed that Patrick had turned deadly white. She herself was too terrified to speak. They sat watching the water, waiting to be destroyed.

"He seems to have gone," said Penelope at last.

There was no answer.

145

"Is that blood in the water?" she asked.

Again there was no reply.

"Patrick!" she shouted.

For answer he flopped back in the canoe and lay with his head by her feet.

"Patrick!" she screamed.

He lay quite still where he had fallen, but she could see that he was breathing. When she touched his shoulder to shake him he moaned.

She was about to dash water in his face, but remembered the shark and hastily drew back her hand. Then she peered over the side, fearful lest she should see the monster still there.

But the morning breeze was already ruffling the surface and nothing was visible below. I suppose we'll drift, she thought, and again she tried to stir Patrick. Each time she touched him he moaned in pain.

Any immediate danger had passed with the disappearance of the shark, and the faint wind was already drifting the canoe along. Penelope remembered the *pareu*, but there was neither spear nor paddle to support it. All she could do was to sit up straight and hold it behind her, as far out on each side as her arms could reach. So, like a bird with scarlet wings, she was carried to the shore.

She had been seen from the land, and a crowd of natives had gathered to watch the strange picture of a pale-skinned girl being borne along by the wind and arriving as it were out of the morning sun.

"*Ia-ora-na!*" they called, as they ran into the water to guide the canoe ashore, *Ia-ora-na* meaning "Hail!"

Then they saw Patrick still lying in the bottom of the canoe where he had fallen.

His eyes opened as the canoe touched land and he sat up, staring in surprise at the crowd about him.

"The shark," Penelope tried to explain; "it attacked us and he drove it away."

They didn't understand.

"It came alongside us," she said, pointing to the water and gesticulating, "it attacked us, and Patrick—"

"*Mai hea mai 'oe?*" asked an old man, meaning in native language: "From where do you come?"

But Penelope went on trying to explain about the shark.

"*Parlez français?*" asked a girl standing by her.

"A little," said Penelope, "I mean *peu—un peu.*"

"*D'où venez-vous?*" the girl asked.

Penelope knew that this meant where had they come from, but she couldn't think how to answer. She could only point into the sun in the direction of Paheero's island.

"*Le soleil, ils viennent du soleil,*" exclaimed the girl.

"*Ariki!*" whispered someone, meaning chief. "*Ariki, te ariki,*" was muttered all around. The crowd drew back, leaving only the old man and the girl who spoke French.

"*Ma'o?*" said the old man, meaning "shark."

"*Avez-vous vu le requin?*" asked the girl.

147

Requin? Penelope could not remember what it meant; but one of the natives was drawing the outline of a shark in the sand with his spear.

"Yes! Yes!" shouted Penelope. "I mean *oui—oui*—shark. Patrick stabbed him with our spear."

"*Pas comprend*," said the girl.

Penelope took the spear and, pointing to Patrick, she stuck it into the drawing of the fish.

"*Ariki, te ariki*," murmured the crowd, "*ariki, te ariki*," they chanted.

The old man advanced to Patrick who was still sitting in the canoe. "*Ariki*," he said, bowing low, "*ariki!*"

Patrick put out his hand in the only gesture of friendship that he knew, but as he raised his arm he winced with pain.

"*Il est blessé*—by the shark," said Penelope, pointing to his shoulder.

At a signal, two young natives approached and lifted him in their arms. Then at the head of a procession, with Penelope close alongside, they carried him to a large native house on the edge of the lagoon. Here they laid him on a soft pile of coconut mats.

All the time the natives who followed were murmuring "*ariki*" and now they stood about in groups whispering "*ariki, te ariki*."

"What do they mean?" Penelope asked the girl. "I mean, *Qu'est-ce qu'ils disent*?"

"*Ils disent que lui, il est ariki, il est le chef*."

"No," said Penelope, "he is—*mon frère*."

"*Votre frère, il est votre frère, vous êtes princesse*?"

"No, my name is Penelope."

"*Comment*?"

"*Mon nom est Penelope*," said she in very bad French.

148

"*Ah, vous vous appelez Panilupé, vous êtes la princesse Panilupé; et votre frère, comment s'appelle-t-il?*"

". . . Don't understand."

"*Votre frère, comment s'appelle-t-il, son nom?*"

"Patrick."

"*Comment?*"

"Pa-trick. *Et vous,*" asked Penelope, "*comment vous appelez-vous?*"

"Vahine," answered the girl.

Meanwhile Patrick had been taken in hand by two old women who were rubbing oil into his dislocated shoulder. After massaging it for a time they fixed a pad of leaves in his armpit, and holding the arm, both above and below the elbow, they moved it gently backwards and forwards until the bone clicked into place.

"*Maitai!*" said one of the old crones, meaning "good!"

"*Maitai!*" said the other.

Then they made a sling for his arm and brought him cool water to drink and gourds full of fruit with which to refresh himself.

Outside the hut there was great activity. Men, women and children passed by, raising their hands and calling "*Ia-ora-na!*"

Only yesterday the old chief had been buried. The service had perforce been conducted by a French priest, but when he was safely out of the way, there came another procession headed by elderly natives who cried out and cut themselves with sharks' teeth until the blood flowed down their faces. They covered the grave with white tapa cloth and laid on it presents of food to sustain the spirit of the dead on its journey to Paradise. In the evening they returned

149

and buried these presents close beside the grave, lest any interfering official might discover that, in spite of the law, there were some who still adhered to ancient customs.

Vahine sat close beside Penelope, whom she had appropriated as her special charge. She knew the old prophecy that one day a chief would die leaving no sons after him, and that a new chief would be born out of the rising sun, that his first act would be to slay a shark, and that he would be carried to the island by scarlet wings.

And it was she herself who had first seen Panilupé—Panilupé, whose name in Tuamotuan meant "bird of the stream", carried thither out of the morning sun holding the red *pareu* outstretched. She was the bird with the scarlet wings, bearing the young chief to land.

Now Vahine remembered stories told her by her father, how other prophecies had come true, how once on a time

Maui the priest had foretold that there would come "*vaa ama ore*", canoes without an outrigger, and "*vaa taura ore*", canoes without ropes, and how all the people had laughed, thinking that no canoe could keep its balance without an outrigger, and that no canoe could sail without ropes. Then the white man had come in his sailing ships without any outriggers, and after that he had come in his steamships without ropes.

"Wish I could understand what they're saying," said Patrick from his couch.

"They think you are the new chief," Penelope told him.

"*Me!*" exclaimed Patrick.

"Yes!"

"What rot, who told you that?"

"Vahine."

"Who's Vahine?"

"She's this native girl. She talks French."

"Can't she talk English?"

"*Parlez-vous anglais?*" Penelope asked her.

"*Non parle anglais, seulement tuamotu et français.*"

"*Est-ce qu'il y a* anyone—what's anyone?" said Patrick, turning to Penelope.

"*Quelqu'un,*" said Penelope.

"*Est-ce qu'il y a quelqu'un parler anglais?*"

"*Non!*" said Vahine, "*pas personne.*"

"Bet they're only ragging," said Patrick.

"Bet they're not. You ask Vahine."

"*Qui est le chef,* Vahine?" he asked.

"*Mais vous, monsieur.*"

"Me! I mean *moi?*"

"*Oui, monsieur,*" she replied.

The noise outside increased, the squealing of pigs could

151

be heard everywhere, men passed by carrying bundles of firewood. Visitors came into the hut bringing presents of hats, mats, rolls of cloth and necklaces of shells.

"There'll be an awful row when they find out who we are," said Patrick.

"Can't you tell them?"

Patrick beckoned to the old man they had first seen on the beach. "*Je ne suis pas un chef,*" he said.

"*Non, monsieur, pas aujourd'hui; mais demain, après la fête, ils vont vous installer.*"

"They're going to crown you tomorrow," said Penelope.

"Not if I can help it."

"I think it would be rather fun."

"Not much fun when they know."

"They couldn't do anything then."

"Couldn't they?"

"Of course not."

"*Voulez-vous quelque chose à manger?*" asked Vahine.

"*Manger?*" said Patrick.

"*Oui, monsieur.*"

"Rather! What have you got?"

"*Pardon, monsieur?*"

"I mean—*qu'avez-vous?*"

"*Qu'en avez-vous,*" corrected Penelope.

"Shut up! She understands. Who's chief anyway?"

"*Voulez-vous du pain?*" said Vahine.

"Bread! I should jolly well think so."

"*Et du café, monsieur?*"

"*Oui, et du beurre et du sucre et du lait.*"

"You sound like a blooming French grammar," said Penelope.

"I wish we had something of *mon oncle,*" said Patrick, "then we wouldn't be in this fix; and I wish to goodness that my shoulder didn't hurt and that we'd stayed at home in England."

"I suppose you'd rather be in the first eleven than be a chief."

"Be a chief? Be a corpse, more like. Go on, tell them before it's too late. I don't want to be stuck with a spear or hit on the head or whatever it is they do."

"Sh-h! Here's more visitors."

Another bale of cloth was laid on the floor and two carved paddles.

"*Ia-ora-na!*"

"*Iorana,*" said Patrick.

Now the drums began to beat. Tum-tum um-tum, tum-tum-um-tum, tum-tum-um-tum.

Vahine brought the coffee. "*Oui, monsieur, une grande fête,*" she said.

CHAPTER FOURTEEN

THE NEW CHIEF MEETS A POET

ALL through that day and all through the night the feasting and dancing was kept up. Every time Patrick fell asleep he was awakened by the beat of drums. If it ceased for one moment it began again the next. Sometimes he dozed, but inevitably a blast of noise brought him back to consciousness.

Earlier in the day he had been led out to the feast, which was held under a long low shelter of coconut fronds decorated with flowers and ferns. Penelope was the only woman to sit down, and each man took his place according to rank, from Otoo, the old man they had first met on the beach, who sat on Patrick's right, to the young men, hardly more than boys, who sat at the far end of the "table".

Before each were placed coconut shells filled with different sauces; wooden bowls called *umetes* served as dishes for the chickens, the pigs, the prawns and lobsters. Taro, yams, breadfruit and sweet potatoes were served on leaves. Each man helped himself, and directly a bowl was emptied it was taken away by the women and refilled.

All the time song and dance went on as an accompaniment to the festivity. Drums, guitars and concertinas added rhythm and colour.

Many of the songs and dances had been specially composed for the occasion and referred to the arrival of their new chief. Girls, fluttering their arms to represent birds, carried a young banana shoot before them, holding aloft for all to see this symbol of new life and a new king.

"*Ca, c'est vous,*" said Vahine in Patrick's ear.

"*Moi?*"

"*Oui, la banane! Demain ils vous installent.*"

Daylight gave way to dusk and still the feast went on. Torches were brought, and in their flickering light the singing, dancing and eating continued.

Patrick's shoulder was stiff and painful, but even so he had eaten till he could hold no more.

"I'm dead with sleep," he said.

"Me too," said Penelope, yawning.

"*Vous voulez dormir?*" whispered Vahine behind them. "*Venez doucement,*" she said, beckoning them to follow.

When they woke next morning, on their piles of mats, Vahine was waiting to bring them coffee—good French coffee in china mugs—and fresh bread and butter. This was indeed civilization again. After that came Mama Hina to massage Patrick's shoulder. By the time she had finished with him he didn't know whether he had a shoulder or not, but the pain had gone and he felt very much better.

"How are we going to get out of this?" he asked Penelope.

"Don't know. What's the matter with it? I think it's fun."

"Blowed if I do."

"It's much better than Paheero's island."

"It'll be much worse when they find out who we are."

"We needn't tell them."

"If we could get to that big island over there we'd probably find McCarthy."

"Do let's stay here a few days and see what happens."

"Oh, shut up, I'm going if I can. You stay if you like, p'raps they'll make you a princess—till they find out."

"What then?"

"You'll be a blooming slave like the other women.

155

You'll be married to one of those fellows at the end of the table last night and you'll spend the rest of your days cooking for him. What's more, you won't be allowed to eat in his presence, jolly well have to wait till he's finished and then have the scraps."

Penelope thought this over and decided that perhaps, after all, it might be as well to move on. But the trouble was that there seemed little chance of getting away. Their own canoe was hauled up close to the village and any attempt to launch it would have been bound to attract attention.

"Don't suppose I can do much with my arm, anyway," muttered Patrick.

But Penelope was quite prepared to paddle across to the main island if only they could get afloat.

Nearly everyone was asleep when they wandered out at midday to explore. Here and there an old woman was pottering about among the houses, and a few small children followed them for a short distance as they went along. Otherwise they saw nobody.

The far side of the island had few houses, but a number of long fishing nets were hanging in the trees to dry. Three canoes were lying close together on the shore. This was their chance.

"Come on, let's pinch one," said Patrick; "pretend we're amusing ourselves if anyone comes along. Here, this one, it's got a spear in it."

Penelope glanced behind to see if all was clear.

"Come on, give a pull."

Slip, slush, splash, into the water went the canoe. Penelope climbed in and took the paddle; Patrick sat astern.

"Go gently," he said, "in case we're seen."

156

From this point of the island to the reef was not more than a few hundred yards, but a wall of coral ran diagonally across and they had to get past this before they could clear the point and head for the big island.

"Keep outside," said Patrick; "the farther the better."

"There's another of these walls near the reef."

"Never mind, keep between them."

"Looks to me as if they were built by hand," said Penelope.

"Go on, I can see a gap."

There was just room for canoe and outrigger to pass between the two weirs.

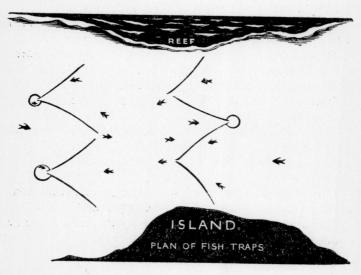

PLAN OF FISH TRAPS

"O.K. Now we're through," said Patrick. "Some game for catching fish, I bet. Keep straight on."

"There's a man on the shore," said Penelope.

"Never mind, take a squint in the water as if we were looking at the fish."

"There's another dam ahead."

"Go on, pretend you're watching the fish and keep outside."

They both tried to appear careless of their direction.

Then another wall appeared on their right.

"Go on, we'll get through, same as before," said Patrick.

"I don't believe we will—can't see a gap."

"Keep her moving."

"Can't make out what these walls are for; I'm sure they're built by hand."

"Fish," said Patrick, "bet you any money it's to catch fish. Look where you're going—whoop!"

The canoe stuck between the two converging barricades.

"Now we're dished," said Patrick.

"It's a kind of a trap," suggested Penelope.

"Caught *us* all right," grunted Patrick, gloomily.

"Can't we lift the canoe over?"

"They're watching us from the shore," he said.

"Who?"

"Two men and a girl."

"That's Vahine," said Penelope.

"Never mind, pretend we don't see her; look in the water, back quietly along and we'll find an opening."

The next time that they looked up they saw a canoe coming towards them.

"*Ia-ora-na,*" called the man in the stern.

"*Iorana,*" said Patrick.

"*Vous cherchez des poissons?*"

"*Non!*"

"*Vous examinez les trappes?*"

Penelope tried to explain that they were admiring the fish but the native could not understand what she meant. After all, the fish were always there and they were always the same. Her remarks had as little meaning for him as if she had told him it was a fine day. Of course it was a fine day, it always is in the Tuamotus, and of course the fish were brightly coloured. They always were. He wondered what she could mean.

But by this time several more canoes had come to join them. Each one held two or three men and a large creel made of plaited bamboo, which the men dropped overboard when they reached the fish trap. A native from each boat then slipped into the water and, with a spear, attacked the numerous fish in the enclosure. It was soon apparent how cleverly the trap had been planned, and how the fish coming in with the current had been guided along by the coral walls until they found themselves in the enclosure at the end. Round and round they went, but each time they approached the entrance their course was changed by a short inward continuation of the weirs. As each fish was speared he was dropped through an opening in the top of a creel, in which he was kept cool and out of the sun.

"Better go back," said Patrick, "and pretend we just went to look at the trap."

Vahine was waiting for them on the shore; and who should be standing alongside her but Tommy, the trader they had met in Tahiti.

"Hullo, you two," he called. "Where's Uncle? Didn't expect to see me here, did you? By golly, you didn't. Uncle —what? Nearly drowned—you're alone on the island? Golly! . . . Who? Paheero, by Jiminee—tell you later. Where's Uncle? On Hikueru you say! Phew, how long you been here—since yesterday?"

"They're going to make Patrick chief," said Penelope.

"They *what*?"

"Make him chief," she repeated.

"*Him*! *Ariki*?"

"*Oui, ariki*," said Vahine.

"Lor', what you been up to?"

"We got here yesterday, and everyone says he is the new chief."

"Hoodely um te doodle!" exclaimed Tommy. "So it was *you* made all the noise last night."

"We didn't make any noise, we couldn't sleep ourselves."

"Bet you didn't, we could hear you at Marama. Old Pa Hinkson, the missionary, was nearly daft with the row, thinks they've all gone savage again."

"Can you get us away?" asked Patrick.

"What! New chief deserting already?"

160

"I'm not a chief."

"Oh, by golly, you are if they say so," said Tommy. "I think you best stay here; if you try run, p'raps they get angry. A spear is very uncomfy in the ribs."

"I can't stay here always," said Patrick.

"Why not?"

"Nothing to do."

"Nothing to do? Who wants to do anything? Wish they'd make me a chief, I'd stay here and do nothing quick enough. We'll see what Sharkie says."

"Sharkie?"

"He's skipper of the *Moana*; that's our schooner lying out there. We came along here find bloke called Tahiri."

"*Vous cherchez Tahiri?*" asked Vahine.

"*Oui, tu le connais?*"

"*Il est mon frère.*"

"*Où est-il?*"

"*Il est parti.*"

"*Parti?*"

Yes, he had gone away to the pearl fishing at one of the other islands where the season had already opened. Tommy was very depressed by this news.

"*Pourquoi vous cherchez Tahiri?*" asked Vahine.

"*Nous allons Tekokoto.*"

"Hullo! hullo!" came the voice of Sharkie. "Have you found Tahiri?"

"No!" answered Tommy, "He's gone pearl diving."

"Blue ants!" said Sharkie as he joined them. "Blue ants and beetles! What do we do now?"

"Go along without him," said Tommy.

"We can't do that!"

"Why not?"

Sharkie sat down and swore. He was an enormous man

with long arms like a monkey's. A pair of wild eyes were half hidden by shaggy eyebrows. When he lifted his hat to wipe his forehead there wasn't a single hair to be seen on his head. His bald, perspiring skull was like an ostrich's egg in a rainstorm.

"Yellow maggots, it's hot—can't stand this leg. Here, you take it off," he said to Patrick, handing him his jack-knife.

Patrick thought he was mad and drew back.

"TAKE IT OFF," he roared, "take it OFF."

"Take what off?" asked Patrick, a bit scared.

" My leg. Cut the string and pull."

"Give it to me," said Tommy, taking the knife. "This is Captain Shanks," he added. "Captain Shanks of the schooner *Moana* meet Penelope and Patrick from London, England. They want to get off the island."

"Get my leg off first," said Sharkie.

On one foot he was wearing a canvas shoe, but from under the trousers on his other leg appeared a leather riding boot tied around with string.

Tommy cut the string and pulled off not only the boot but all that it contained as well.

Sharkie waved the loose leg of his trousers in the air. "Crabs and cuttlefish, how I hate that boot!" He folded the end of his trousers over the stump of his leg and tied it below the knee.

"So Tahiri is gone?" he asked.

"His sister says so."

"His sister?"

"Yes! Vahine over there."

"Vahine? She *his* sister? Give me my foot."

He produced from the sawdust which filled his boot a small bottle of scent.

162

"This will fetch her. *Vahine, te voilà! Tu veux du parfum?*" he called.

Vahine jumped to her feet and ran towards them. "*Mais oui, monsieur. Merci! Oo la-la!*" she said, as she poured some of the contents on the fern wreaths she had been plaiting.

Then they talked away in native language, and every now and again Sharkie slapped his thigh.

"She knows the spot, by golly she knows the spot," said Tommy, "and she's a diver too. I tell you, we'll get those pearls and we'll swallow the anchor and live ashore."

"Where are these pearls?" asked Patrick.

"In the *Toroa*, in the captain's cabin, hundreds of 'em, big as your fist, all from the same reef, new reef, no one knows where. Old man Brown, the skipper, always messin' about the atolls, he'd take his ship where you couldn't float a cork. One day he finds little lagoon, cram jam full of shell, big bluelipped ones. Golly, they held pearls! Most shell hold nothing; most divers lucky find one or two small pearls in a day, lucky find one big one in the year, but old Brown had enough to go twice round the fat woman at the circus. If he hadn't got on that reef he could have bought the Pacific."

"Rats alive! Come back to the ship," roared Sharkie.

He was standing on his one leg clutching a tree. Seizing Patrick and Tommy by the shoulders he used them as a pair of crutches and progressed across the island in a series of prodigious hops.

"Archangels and peacocks, we're rich," he roared. Vahine followed them with the empty boot.

> "*Don't forget the boot,*
> *We'll fill it up with loot.*

163

"I'm a poet," he said to Patrick. "Aren't I a poet, Tommy?"

"Best in the Pacific!" said Tommy.

"That's right, poet of the Pacific. When I go ashore I'll write poems all day long.

> *"Poems of the sea*
> *About Tommy and me.*

"It's easy, the words fall out.

> *"Green and yellow maggots*
> *Feed on rotten carrots,*
> *But white mice*
> *Don't think them nice."*

"You're cracking my neck," said Tommy.

The natives were a little surprised when they saw their new chief being used as a stilt by this old ruffian who was well known on the island, and many of them followed the party to the shore.

When Sharkie heaved himself on board the surf boat and was followed by Tommy, Patrick, Penelope and Vahine, they merely thought it was a friendly visit to the ship. Not until the schooner swung with the wind and headed for the pass in the reef, did they realize that their new chief had departed as suddenly as he had arrived.

CHAPTER FIFTEEN

A SCOTSMAN, AN IRISHMAN AND
AN AMERICAN

WHILE these events had been happening to the children, matters had not gone very much better for their uncle.

After being capsized at the entrance to the lagoon, an undercurrent had carried him back into deep water where he was very nearly drowned. When, however, half suffocated, he did manage to come to the surface, he was able to grasp the gunwale of their boat floating near by. She was right way up and full of water and he succeeded in clambering over the side, but, in her waterlogged condition, she could hardly support his weight. Each time he moved she lurched, and he expected at any moment to be upset again.

He could see the children lying on the shore, but he was unable to make his voice heard against the noise of the surf. The boat bobbed this way and that. One moment it was being rushed towards the reef, the next it was being carried out to sea. His right leg was numb and the slightest movement caused him intense agony. Even so he would have tried to swim but that he knew he would be smashed on the reef.

There was no sign of the oars. Everything had fallen out except the wooden scoop used as a bailer, and this, tied to a thwart, was floating beside him. He tried to make use of it, but the water lapped in almost as quickly as he could get it out.

Meanwhile the current had been carrying him along, and by the time a rain squall had passed the children were out of sight, hidden by a curve in the reef. He had seen enough to know that, at any rate, they were alive. Several times he decided to try to get ashore, but the pain in his leg, which he now realized was broken, made the attempt impossible.

By the time he dared to relax his efforts at bailing it was already dark, and the current setting away from the point of the island carried him farther and farther to sea. But at any rate he had got the boat fairly clear of water, and away from the reef the sea wasn't quite so choppy. There was nothing to do but lie down in his wet clothes and try to sleep; then he remembered Amundsen's prophecy of a storm. It wasn't a very cheering thought.

Each time he began to doze, he was brought back to consciousness by spray in his face or by squalls of rain. Sometimes a wave would slap the side of the boat, making him think he had struck land. He was chilled and utterly miserable. What were the children doing? Was there any food for them on the island? How would the natives treat them? They'd probably have some of the stores washed up. Hope they weren't hurt. Silly to have tried to land . . . Old Amundsen ought to have known better. How *could* they wait for the wave? Didn't have a chance . . . How would he face old Mary at home if anything happened to them? P'raps he ought to have swum. No good! That surf would have finished him. How awful that face of the reef had looked, worse than barbed wire entanglements in the war.

He tried to turn over on to his side, but the pain in his leg prevented him. He stared up at the stars. The Southern Cross, supposed to be beautiful—not much in it, he thought, just four stars in the shape of a diamond. He wished to goodness he could see the good old Plough and the North Star and—oh, how he wished he could go to sleep.

He did eventually drop off, and when he woke it was to see a couple of white men and a crowd of natives looking down at him over the side of a schooner.

"Hey, but yer looking far thro'," said the captain. "Can a man no gie ye a haund?"

"Damaged my leg, can't move!"

"That's aw right! We hae a medical man aboard. Up wi' 'im, twa o' ye. Come on, Mister Murphy, here's something fer ye noo!"

"You've got a tidy few bruises, haven't ye now?" said the doctor, as he tied up his leg and changed him into dry clothes.

"Expect I hit something down below."

"Coral," said Dr. Murphy. "Don't be goin' in the salt water till them cuts are after healing, or ye'll have reefs growing on yer shins."

"I can't move far with these splints, anyway."

168

"Arrah, stay where you are, there's nothing to be moving for."

"The children on the island!"

"Make yer mind easy, sure the island is teeming with everything in the world and there's the nicest, quietest, decentest native ever you met livin' up there. He'll feed them and he'll house them and he'll wash them, and next time he wants a drop of drink he'll take them down across the lagoon to the big island beyond."

"We were hoping to find a chap called MacCarthy, an author," said Uncle John.

"Ah sure, poor Mac, he's daft, a touch of the sun I think; spends all his time chasin' fish and wondering what the coral reef is made of. One day he says it's volcanoes that have grown up, and the next time you see him 'tis islands that have gone down. Sure I was at school with poor Larry, he was the grandest shot in the world till he gave up shooting. I tell ye he could hit a bird that wasn't there with a blank cartridge! Faith, one day he threw away his gun,' 'Tis a pity,' he says, 'to be taking pleasure in hurting the poor little things. I'd rather watch them,' he says—there, are ye more comfortable now? Ye're what? Ye're cold? Wait a while till I see if I can squeeze a drop of comfort out of old Jock."

" 'Twas no ill wind fer that man that took us oot a' oor course," said the captain, coming along with a bottle. "There's nae doot 'tis a handy thing at times, yon wireless. I'm thinkin' the storm's gied awa' sooth."

"I suppose the doctor's fees come out of that bottle too," said Murphy. "Indeed, I'll be starting a sanatorium now wid me one patient."

That evening, towards dusk, they landed at Hikueru, and

Alexander was carried to the doctor's house. It was one large, cool room, walled in with bamboos and roofed with pandanus and divided into three sections by screens of coconut matting.

At one end was the doctor's bedroom, at the other his surgery, and in the middle the sitting-room. At the back was a separate cookhouse in which native women were preparing food. Alexander was allotted the sitting-room and was soon furnished with the only bed in the place.

"I tell you what it is," said Murphy, "I could sleep on drawing pins; I'm that used to queer places, I'm only comfortable when I'm uncomfortable, I haven't slept in a bed for months. When ye're in Rome do as Rome does: when ye're in Dublin visit Guinness's brewery, and when ye're in the South Seas 'tis better for ye sleep on mats."

"I'm worried about those children," said Alexander.

"What are ye worried about? Didn't I tell you they were safer there than they would be in London itself, not a motor to run over them, not a person to do them a ha'p'orth of harm; they can lie down and sleep where they like and the food is lying around them like a harvest thanksgiving. 'Tis a picnic they're on, the finest they'll ever have."

"I ought to get back."

"Well, if you had the two legs under ye and a hundred pounds in yer pocket ye couldn't get back, for there's no schooner goin' out of this for weeks. D'ye think I'd be lettin' ye go off in a canoe, with a broken leg and a temperature near boilin' point? 'Tis better for you rest easy where ye are and be thankful yer not floatin' about like an empty bottle the way ye were this morning."

"You're sure they're all right?"

"If I was as sure of Heaven, I'd die happy this minute."

"Can't go tonight anyway, I suppose," said Alexander.

"Drink this and forget about it," said Murphy. "I'll make enquiries in the morning; maybe there'll be a launch, or the like of it, would go and fetch them for you."

But Alexander couldn't forget about it, and as he lay there with aching leg and throbbing head, he pictured to himself every possible tragedy that might have happened. He was in a high state of fever; one moment bathed in perspiration, the next, even in that heat, shivering all over.

Murphy sat by him filling his glass with whisky. "The more of that ye put inside of ye the quicker ye'll be cool," he said, "and the quicker ye're cool the quicker ye'll be warm again."

"I've never been so hot in my life," said Alexander.

"No, an' ye were never so cold in yer life as ye were five minutes ago. For the love of Heaven keep that blanket over ye."

The hours went by and there was no sleep for either of them. Alexander waved his arms and muttered. He tried to get up, but was stopped by the pain in his leg. At intervals the doctor bathed his face and hands with cold water, and when the shivering fits came on he covered him with an extra blanket. Eventually Alexander dropped into a heavy sleep.

When he woke, it was early morning and everybody was moving about. "What time is it?" he asked.

"Faith, it's the day after tomorrow," said Murphy.

"The what?"

"The day after tomorrow. D'ye know how long ye've slept?"

"Four or five hours, I suppose."

"Twenty-four or five hours and a little bit over."

"What about the children?"

"They're safe enough. How are you feelin' yerself?"

"Pretty limp."

"And ye will be for a day or two after the fever ye had. Wait a while till old mama brings a cup of tea and ye'll be a different man. . . . There! Are ye better now?" he said as he propped him up.

"Was I really asleep all that time?" asked Alexander.

"Faith, if you weren't, you'd 'a been dead with the way you were goin' on, shoutin' and kickin' and roarin'. Will you look at the colour of my nose?"

"It's a bit blue," said Alexander.

"A bit blue is it, 'twas purple and puce it was yesterday with the wallop you caught me."

"Me?"

"Yes, you, bang on the tip with your clenched fist, just as I was bein' a mother to ye, tuckin' ye in and all that. Three o'clock in the morning—I could see me watch with the stars ye knocked out of me."

"I'm frightfully sorry," said Alexander.

"Well, ye're not more sorry than I was meself, but ye're no worse than the rest. The last time I took out a tooth, the

fellow hit me in the stomach as I was bendin' over him. D'ye see them carved paddles on the wall? 'Twas a present he brought me afterwards to show he was sorry."

"I'll have to try and make up for it too," said Alexander.

"That's easy enough, just sit still and let me talk to you. D'ye think I'm not glad to have a man in the house I can talk to, d'ye think I'm not glad to hear the sound of me own language? Me livin' alone and hearin' nothing but 'native', day in, day out."

"Well, I seem to be here whether you like it or not."

"Drink your tea, man, don't be talking!"

"The place is seething," said Murphy. "You'd have more rest inside of an ants' nest. They've come for the pearling from every island in the group, from Fakarava and Takaroa over in the west, and from Hao and Amanu and Papakaua in the east, and from every other speck of coral that holds a palm tree. Houses galore, look at 'em, not one there last week. Flies isn't in it, crabs isn't in it—thousands of 'em, all in their own little villages. There's a cinema party comin' to take pictures—what d'ye think of that?"

"They might lend me their ship," said Alexander.

"They'll be presentin' you with a coffin if ye don't lie quiet and rest."

"I couldn't move if I wanted to."

"And what were you doin' when I came in a while ago?"

"Only watching a schooner come in."

"Oh, that's old Sleath, wait a while till I go and have a word with him."

As Murphy truly said, the place was alive. Natives had come from all the surrounding islands and were camping in hastily built palm shelters. A service in the church next morning would open the pearling season, and then the launches and cutters would be seen towing long strings of canoes across the lagoon to the diving grounds.

During the day a party of Americans arrived in a yacht. It wasn't a cinema company after all, but just a few men come to take shots of any local colour which could not be produced in Hollywood. All the diving scenes and the underwater fights with sharks could be photographed much

173

better and more safely at home. What they wanted was merely to see how things were done, and to collect a few oddments of native manufacture to give an air of reality to their "sets".

"Say, boy! Where'd you get that stool!" said Arthur P. Henniker. "Gee, that's swell, the finest stool I seen in the Islands, must be five foot long."

"Four foot nine," said Murphy; "three foot across and two foot six high, all cut out of one solid block. It was given to me by an old chief—same time he gave me his appendix."

"Why, I thought myself pretty smart to find one twelve inches by four."

"'Tis a pillow you've got, not a seat."

"A pillow?"

"Nothing else. Got any drums?" asked Murphy.

"Don't worry! I'm O.K. there. I got two, one of 'em's three foot high, made of a hollow tree and a shark-skin top."

"Maybe you won't believe me when I tell you 'twas eight foot long they used to be and two foot across, and the drummer had to stand on a platform. Them was the drums to put the fear into your heart. Two o'clock in the morning, or three, they'd start. You wouldn't sleep too easy in your bed with the like of that going on. Maybe 'twas yourself would be the sacrifice they wanted. Have ye got any of the little bamboo drums with the hole in them?"

"Where can I see those?"

"Faith, you can see them and hear them any night you like down here. Just a bit of the tree with the sections left in at each end and a slit down the side. Grand music they make with a stick. And the conchs?"

"Say! I've got a couple of swell shells, but I can't blow 'em."

"Maybe you haven't filed off the tips? You have? Well, you're not holding your mouth properly. You must blow with your lips pressed up same as you would into a brass cornet, then you'll be heard all over America."

During the days that followed, Henniker dropped in each evening with news of his latest acquisitions: shells, loosely woven for necklaces, and closely woven for hatbands; house brooms made out of the midribs of coconut leaflets; carved wooden bowls ornamented with mother of pearl. He wanted to find some of the wooden mallets for beating the bark of trees into tapa cloth. He wanted to find some of the stone or coral pounders used for preparing the taro.

Murphy was always ready with a better story than anyone else. "Towed by a shark you were in your yacht! How would you like to be in a canoe and to be towed by a devil fish? Six yards long and ten yards wide and weigh a ton. Like a great flat skate they are, with a tail like a whip and a pair of horns on their heads like a cow, and they lepping out of the water and sailing about in the air like a bird."

"Have another drink and tell us it had a neck like a giraffe and could speak Irish."

"I'm telling you the truth, five and six feet they leap, and when they fall back in the water, 'tis like the report of a cannon. Try harpooning one of them and ye'll find motor boats slow travelling ever after."

175

"I wish you'd find me a motor boat," said Alexander.
"How many more times will I tell you that there isn't
a plank of wood will stir out of this for another week?
Wait a while till they're packed up with shell and a few
pearls hidden away in the heels of their shoes, or inside
their cigars, like poor Dunne. What, ye didn't hear about
him? Sure the whole town was laughing, all except Dunne.
'I'm Dunne by name and done by nature', says he. Sure he
hid a big pearl in a cigar, thinking to smuggle it through—
and if he didn't mix up his cigars and give the wrong one to
the customs officer!"

"What did the customs officer say?"

"Faith, he didn't say anything except that his wife was
waitin' for him and he must be goin'—pretended he hadn't

found it at all, never said a word more, and there was poor Dunne couldn't say a word either."

"What did the officer do with it?"

"Sold it to be sure, smuggled it himself. Forty pounds he got for it, and all he did was stand Dunne a drink."

"I'll tell you what," said Henniker, getting up; "if you can't get out of this in a week I'll help you along to Marama in the yacht."

CHAPTER SIXTEEN
A VISIT TO MARAMA

"SAY, boy, how long'll it take you to pack your suit case?" asked Henniker a few evenings later. "We've got all the stuff we can use from here. How about paying a call on those children of yours?"

"Ready in five minutes," said Alexander.

"Can he go, Doc?"

"He can if he's carried and if he don't put foot under him, and if he keeps out of small boats and swimming races."

"First thing in the morning," said Henniker, "the boys will come for you."

"Fill yer glass," said Murphy. "Where are ye going after Marama—back to Hollywood?"

"Back to Tahiti; Duprès's coming with us."

"Oho, ye've got the police wid ye! Who is he after now?"

"No one at all; he's leaving Lefroy to take charge."

"Just goin' for a little holiday, I suppose. Well, God help us, the poor fellow has done nothin' long enough, I suppose it's time he had a rest!"

"Got any message for MacCarthy if we find him?" asked Alexander.

"Tell him he's right after all, same as Darwin was: 'tis on the tops of sunken mountains that the coral grows. Tell him I seen a review in the papers a while back. And, whisper, tell him I'll be in Tahiti when the diving is over."

"There's only one thing I'm sorry about," said Murphy next morning when he was saying goodbye to Alexander.

"And that?"

"That ye didn't break both of yer legs and the pair of yer arms and a couple of ribs. Then, maybe I'd have had yer company a while longer."

"And I'd have been more in your debt than ever," said Alexander.

"Debt, debt, did ye say? And me starving to hear a man speak the King's English? What do ye think I do sittin' here day after day, waiting for a man to be eaten by a shark, waiting to tie up an arm that's been bitten off by a barracuda. I tell you the bones in me behind makes holes in the chairs, and the sweat of me head makes lakes on the floor, an' me readin' a paper is six months old."

At the last moment something went wrong on the yacht, and they didn't get away till the afternoon. They arrived at Marama and entered the north pass in the lagoon about noon on the following day. Henniker went ashore to try to find news of the children.

"They're safe enough," he said when he got back. "The whole island is talking about them—just gone off with a couple of guys, Tommy and Sharkie, in the *Moana*."

179

"Where to?" asked Alexander, anxiously.

"Nobody knows."

"Back to Tahiti, p'raps?"

"Everyone's got a different yarn."

"And MacCarthy?"

"He's gone off to Tahiti."

While they were waiting for some fruit from the shore, a native paddled out and came on board.

"You lookin' for two white boys?" he asked.

"Boy and a girl," said Alexander.

"Same thing. They pinch my canoe."

"Where are they now?"

"Don't know, hopped it in schooner. You Uncle John?" he asked.

"Yes, I'm Uncle John; and you?"

"I'm Paheero. How much you pay me for *pirogue* they steal, and how much you pay me all food they eat?"

"How do I know they pinched your canoe?"

"'Cause I tell you, 'cause I say they come along eat everything on island," said Paheero.

"What do *you* think?" said Alexander to Duprès, who was dozing in a deck chair with his hat over his eyes. "Can we take his word as evidence?"

Duprès sat up, blinked his eyes and scratched his head. At sight of his face Paheero turned and took a flying jump into the water. By the time they had reached the side of the yacht he was out of view. Not a sign of him to be seen.

"Dived under," said Alexander, crossing the deck. "Yes, there he goes! That's quick work."

Paheero in his canoe was paddling full speed for the shore.

180

"Not very glad to see me," said Duprès, the police officer. "I *seem* to remember his face in Court."

Three days later they reached Tahiti. Yes, MacCarthy was back at his house at Arué and had bought the old wreck which lay in the lagoon. "Grandest aquarium in the world," he said; "water in and out through the cracks all day. Look at the fish, happy as fleas."

MacCarthy was exactly as Tommy had described him, like a fish. No chin, a pointed nose and protruding eyes. He ran about with short, quick steps as if he were darting from rock to rock below the surface of a pool. Fish were the ruling passion of his life, and he only considered coral because it was the home of his more brightly coloured

favourites. The house in which he lived was built out into the lagoon and all around it were tanks and cages, ingeniously arranged, so that the water was always fresh and the lighting such that he himself could see without being seen.

For hours each day he would sit under water with a

clothes peg on his nose and one end of a hose pipe in his mouth; the other end which admitted air was fastened to a float. He didn't possess as much as a bone or one tooth of a dead fish: his whole interest was to see them alive and watch their movements and behaviour. It was his boast that he had never, in his studies, consciously injured as much as a fin of one of them, and yet he knew more than most of the scientists whose houses were filled with skeletons and pathetic specimens preserved in spirit.

The queer thing was that even on a strange island the fish instinctively knew that there was nothing to fear from him. He never went into the water without taking a mouthful of coconut which he chewed up and spat into the water, so that, as he went along, he was not unlike a comet with a long trail of brightly coloured atoms following in his wake.

Alexander had got rid of his splints and was busy filling book after book with sketches of MacCarthy's guests. No specimen stayed in the cages for more than a day; after that they were sent off to play with their fellows in the open lagoon. Many a drawing was left unfinished because the "model's" time was up.

"What right have we to make them unhappy?" asked MacCarthy. "Isn't it bad enough that we spend most of our lives shut up in prisons of our own making? No fish spends more than twenty-four hours in my company unless he wants to. Of course, some of them like it: that red grouper over there, he comes along regularly, just whenever he's a bit hungry. Sometimes I have to *drive* him out so that he'll take exercise and not get lazy."

Uncle John gave MacCarthy the message from Murphy.

"Of course, Darwin's right," said MacCarthy; "how else could it happen? Reef-forming corals can't live below two hundred feet. How could they grow up from the

bottom? And the lagoons with the reef all round them—
look!" he said, "give me that pencil, it's as clear as daylight." He began to draw diagrams.

"(A) Tall island, coral grows round the edge and makes
a fringing reef.

"(B) Island is slowly sinking. All the islands round here
sank at one time, slowly of course, took thousands of years.
Coral growing all the time, but growing quickest at its
outer edge where there's most food from the open sea.
Now, you see, you've got a barrier reef with lagoon
between it and the land, same as we're on here in Tahiti.

"(C) Island sunk below sea and coral grown right over

it—there's your atoll. Sticks and leaves get washed up and rot into soil, sand worms chew up the coral and make mud; then one day a coconut floats along, digs in its toes, and there's the first palm."

"I always thought it was the craters of sunken volcanoes that made atolls that shape," said Alexander.

"Likely enough it was, here and there, but you couldn't have thousands of volcanoes dotted all over the place, like the Tuamotus."

"Not with safety!" said Alexander.

CHAPTER SEVENTEEN

BY GOLLY IT'S TRUE!

"WHY didn't Captain Brown go back for his pearls?" asked Patrick, when the *Moana* was safe at sea.

"'Cos he died," said Tommy, "and all the crew was drowned."

"How did anyone know about it, then?"

"Captain was picked up in boat, told 'em the story afore he died."

"Can't think why someone didn't go after them," said Patrick.

"The *Toroa* was sunk too deep. That's the secret! By golly that's the secret. She's not deep any more. No, by Jiminee, that last storm threw her up; she's in shallow water now."

"How do you know that?"

"I'll tell you—listen! I was in Kelly's bar on Wednesday, and three chaps off a schooner were sitting there drinking. One of them starts telling a story about a bird they couldn't shoot. 'A duck,' he says; 'I tell you 'twas a duck and 'twas swimming close in and, as we passed, the skipper takes a sight with his rifle and fires. Never a move out of the bird though the bullet splashed close behind him. Then he fired again and the splash was in front. "He's asleep", said the captain. Then Tahiri takes a shot and blows the head off the bird, but it goes on swimming same as ever.' That was the end of the story. By Jiminee, they all laughed and each of 'em tried to pitch a better yarn.

"*Now!* Listen to me," said Tommy, lowering his voice

185   G

and growing confidential; "that bird is carried on the mast-head of the *Toroa*. I know it, by golly, I do! *Toroa* is native name for wild duck. 'Twas down there she was wrecked. That ship has been lifted by the storm, or I'm a clam. There's a packet of pearls waiting for us."

"Whose schooner is this we're on?" asked Penelope.

"Why, Sharkie's! He's captain. Old pal of mine, bit rough, but a good scout. Listen! When I hear that yarn in the bar I nip along, and where do you think I find him?"

"In his bath?"

"No fear, not him."

"In jail?"

"Wrong again. I'll tell you: in the Queen's palace, that's where he was, waiting to present a poem to Her Majesty."

"Sharks and catfish! What you fellows talking about?" said Sharkie, as he flopped on the deck beside them. By the use of a few extra ropes strung about the ship, he was as nimble with his two arms and one leg as most people would be with their full complement of limbs.

Now he swung himself alongside them and rested the stump of his leg on one of the numerous wooden brackets he had fixed in various places.

"Tell them how you lost your foot," said Tommy.

"What about my hair?" asked Sharkie.

"Same story," said Tommy.

> "*I didn't care a hoot*
> *To lose my foot.*

"That's a bad rhyme!" said Sharkie.

> "*But I couldn't just bear*
> *To lose my hair.*

"That's a better one."

186

"Go on, tell them," said Tommy.

"Ever been hungry?" said Sharkie to Penelope.

"Yes, often."

"Let me sit down. When?"

"When we landed on the island and only had eggs and coconut."

"*Only* eggs and coconut! What else do you want on an island—roast peacocks and passion fruit?"

"We had nothing else for days," said Penelope.

"Nothing else! How would you like to eat trouser buttons—trouser buttons and stones, nothing else for days?"

"You couldn't eat those?"

"No, but you could suck 'em to keep your mouth moist."

"Did *you* ever do that?" asked Patrick.

"Did I ever? Listen to him! Did I ever. *Me! Sharkie.* Did I ever? Yes, I did! Where was that, did you say? Where was that? I'll tell you; right in the middle of this 'ere Pacific Ocean."

"Yes! By golly it was," said Tommy.

"Shut up," said Sharkie, "I'm telling this story. He must butt in," he said to the children, "can't let a man tell his own story. Where was I?"

"Middle of the Pacific," said Tommy.

"That's right, middle of the Pacific, right in the middle of this blooming ocean and two weeks without food or drink."

"Didn't you catch any rain?" said Tommy.

"Shut up! I'm coming to that. He can't keep quiet," said Sharkie. "As I was saying," he continued, "right in the middle of this 'ere ocean, with no drop of water but the rain we could squeeze out of our shirts."

"Blooming scandal!" said Tommy.

187

"Blooming scandal? Blooming starvation! Blooming murder! Do you know what the owner of that schooner had done? He'd packed her up tight with old iron, old beds, old bicycles, bits of old motor cars; and he'd insured her hard. Thousands and thousands of pounds, and she didn't carry a hundred francs' worth all told."

"What did he tell the captain?" asked Tommy.

"*Can't* you keep quiet? Who's telling this story?" roared Sharkie. "As I was saying, what do you think the owner told the captain?"

"That's what *I* was saying," said Tommy.

"There'll be an accident on this ship before long," said Sharkie, looking at Tommy. "What he said was: 'Take this rotten old schooner to the farthest island in the archypelgo—' "

"*Pel-a-go*," said Tommy.

"Shut up! . . . 'the farthest island,' he said, 'and sink her. We'll go snags in the insurance,' he said."

"What did the captain say?"

"He didn't say anything, what could he say? He didn't know that half the planks in her bottom was sawn through and the other half had strong acid poured on them to rot 'em."

"A dirty trick!"

"Of course 'twas a dirty trick! Who's telling this story? As I was saying, we were hardly outside the reef when she began to leak. Next day a gale comes up from south-east, the rudder jams, and when we try to force it, it falls off and we're blown away north of Tetioroa, miles and miles to sea."

"What do you think of that for a happy picnic?" said Tommy.

"Don't think about it! Listen! Suddenly we find she's

half-full of water, the rotten bottom had stove in. Hardly time to launch the boat, nothing in her when we did, no oars, no anything except an axe and an old shark hook and a bit of rope."

"Wasn't there any food in the boat?" asked Patrick.

"'Course there wasn't, we weren't an Atlantic liner or a pleasure cruiser. I tell you there was nothing, no food, no anything. All we could do was do nothing; just sit there and

die of hunger. If it hadn't been for the captain's swearing we'd 'a caught a chill. Angels and Innocents, how he did swear! We thought he'd set the blinking boat on fire. All that day we sat there and all the next and the next after that again. We hadn't got a mast and we hadn't got a sail. One night a flying fish hit a man in the face and dropped into the open neck of his shirt. There it was, flapping against his skin, and he too scared to see what it was. Gee-hosh-u-phat, it didn't stay there long. Bones, fins, head,

189

guts and all; that was the only food we had for a whole bloomin' fortnight."

"Didn't anyone die?" asked Tommy.

"*Nobody* died," said Sharkie, "and you know it. Old Aporo the cook wished he was dead.

" 'You will be soon,' said the captain.

" 'No, I won't!' shouted Aporo. 'If any man touches me,' he said, picking up the axe, 'I'll brain him.' Then we knew he was scared he'd be eaten and that put notions in our heads.

"Next day the captain says he thinks we'll starve, the whole lot of us, he says, unless we take a chance on it.

" 'A chance on it?' we asked.

" 'Yes,' he says, 'there's five of us in the boat and it's a five to one chance.'

" 'It's a dead snip,' said somebody.

" 'It isn't,' he says, 'it's *five to one*.' You should have seen their faces when they knowed what he meant. 'Five to one,' he says, 'is good odds.'

" 'Tomorrow!' says somebody.

" 'Yus, tomorrow,' says somebody else, so we leave it at that.

"You should have seen us that day, each one eyeing the other, trying to think who was the least bony. Every time we looked up there was a greedy eye fixed on us. I could see they was all thinking of me 'cos I was the biggest and they thought I'd go further. No one spoke a word and everyone was scared to go to sleep that night. Next morning we wus all nearly dead with fright anyway.

" 'Five to one,' says the captain, soon after dawn.

" 'Tomorrow,' says someone.

" 'Five to one,' says the captain again.

" 'Put it off,' says old Billy.

190

" 'We'll all be dead tomorrow,' said the captain.

" 'Let's wait for the first.'

" 'Five to one,' said the captain.

"Then we agreed, and the old man takes a handful of cash out of his pocket. 'Anyone got any more coins?' he says. Yes, we most of us had a few.

" 'Throw 'em in the hat,' he says.

"Then he shook 'em all together and folded the hat so no one could see inside. 'Now,' he says, 'whoever draws the oldest coin—he's for it'."

"Bet your hands were shaky," said Tommy.

"Our *whole bodies* was shaky. I tell you our teeth was making more rattle than the coins in the hat.

" 'No fumbling,' says the captain. 'Draw your coin and lay it on the thwart.'

"He keeps rattling the hat as each one puts his hand in. Then he gave Aporo the hat and drew one himself.

" 'Mine's 1912,' he says. 'Who beats that?'

" '1917,' said Aporo, showing his coin.

" 'You're out,' said the captain.

" '21,' said the boy.

" 'Out,' said the captain.

"Then he looks at me. 'What's yours?' he said.

" 'Double o!' said I.

" 'What?' says he, and they were all looking hard at me.

" 'Nineteen hundred,' said I, with my voice cracking and my stomach rattling.

"Old Billy had fainted, and was lying with his coin clenched in his hand.

" 'Give us his coin,' said the captain.

"It was 1900, the same as me own.

" 'A tie,' said the captain.

" 'Draw again,' said I.

191

" 'No fear,' said everyone, 'it's you or Bill.'

" '*He's* good as dead anyway,' said Aporo, who was always a friend of mine.

" 'Fair doos,' said the captain. 'Toss for it.'

"Bill had opened his eyes and seemed surprised to find himself still in the same world.

" 'You call, Bill, when he tosses.'

"Murdering Maria! You should have seen me try to fix that coin on my thumb. Twice it fell in the boat; then, at last, I got it in the air. Bill sits up with a start and calls heads; the boat gives a lurch and the coin bounces off the gunwale into the water."

"That was luck," said Tommy.

"Bad luck!" said Sharkie. "It might have been him.

"Then the captain says, 'Do it again.'

" 'Draw from the hat,' says someone.

"Old Bill put out his hand and took a coin. 'Thirteen,' he says, '1913!' Then he fainted again.

"When I put my hand in that hat every coin seemed red hot; my fingers was that swelled up, I couldn't get a grip on them, and when I did pull one out 'twas 1883, the very year I was born."

"Fate!" said Tommy.

"No one spoke a word," said Sharkie. "Then everyone shifted away, leaving me alone in the bow.

" 'It's you,' says the captain.

"They was all looking first at the axe and then at me, then at the axe again, and I wondered when they was going to start.

" 'How long have I got?' said I.

"No one answered.

" 'How long have I got?' I asked again.

" 'This evening,' said the captain.

"That was better than I hoped; maybe a ship would come along. Angels of Heaven, how I spiered that empty horizon.

"Not a ship, not a mast, not a cloud, not even a bird; only the water, smooth as oil."

"A nice day before you," said Tommy.

"A nice five years," said Sharkie; "I tell you, every hour of that day was like a week. Yes, and when I looks over the side there's a shark come to join us. You know what that means!"

"Sharks know when they're going to be fed," said Tommy.

"I tell you, it *was* cheerful, sittin' there with them blood-shot eyes lookin' at me, and wondering which part of me they'd start on.

"Then I thinks of me prayers, but I don't shut no more'n one eye for fear of that axe, and I prays, Halleleujah how I prayed! Any sort of a ship, O Lord, any sort of old ship, so long as she has food on board.

"Then I looked all round the horizon; no, not even a puff of smoke from a funnel.

"Then I pray again and say, O Lord, can't you send us some flying fish; not one, O Lord, inside a man's shirt, but whole flocks, O Lord, in the bottom of the boat.

"Then I sits up and waits for the flying fish, but nothing breaks the surface of the sea, nothing—except that shark's fin.

"Then I pray again and say, O Lord, if you could save Jonah from the whale, can't you save poor Shanks from this boatload of cannibals?

"While I'm thinking about Jonah I hear them whispering to themselves. 'Catch shark tomorrow,' says someone.

"Yes, I says to myself, and I know very well the bait

193   G*

you'll be using. When they see me looking at them they stop talking.

"Then I pray again and I say, 'O Lord, can't you find some other bait than me for that dam' shark?' I tell you I *was* miserable, my feet was like frozen beef and when I scratched my head all the hair fell out."

"He had lovely hair once," said Tommy.

"So I goes on praying and praying like mad. I say more prayers in one hour than a bishop says in ten years. Then I get a sudden thought and I say to the captain, 'If my leg'll be good for bait tomorrow when I'm dead, why not a bit of it now? Then p'raps no need to do me in.'

" 'What do you mean?' he says.

" 'Take my foot,' I said. 'Take my foot and let me keep the rest.'

" 'Quite right,' said Aporo; 'good fellow, old Shanks, we'll catch shark with his foot.'

"So the captain and all the others swear, if I give my foot and they catch the shark they won't do me in.

"Then I lie down and the captain ties strips of his shirt tight round my leg, and he puts a bit of shirt over my face, and he holds my hand and he swears he'll stand by me.

"Then I feel a crack on my shin, but my leg's so numb I don't feel very much; then I get another crack and I pray, 'O Lord, don't forget that shark,' then my leg burns and hurts and then I seem to swim away, and I don't know any more till I find something trickling down my throat and I see Captain and Aporo squeezin' a bit of flesh over my mouth."

"Did they really catch the shark?" asked Patrick.

"*Course* they did. Fastened my foot to the hook and dropped it overboard with a splash; if they hadn't lashed the rope to a thwart they'd all 'a been pulled overboard.

194

It took 'em hours to tire that shark, and then they had to slosh him on the head with the axe before they could bring him on board.

"Two days later we was picked up by a mail boat from San Francisco; regular heroes we were. The doctor fixed my leg and the ladies and gents all subscribed and gave us fifty quid in cash. Now everyone calls me Sharkie."

"Did they find your foot inside the shark?"

"You bet they did! I've got the bones at home—they make a nice rattle for the kids."

CHAPTER EIGHTEEN

GENTLE AS A LAMB!

THEY were not due at their island until the following morning, and as they bounced along with the south-east "trade" on their beam Tommy enquired about their life at Marama.

"You're mighty lucky you didn't have anything worth pinching; that fellow Paheero would have had it in two tics. He'd pinch the soles off your feet and you walking in glue."

"He was very nice till he got drunk," said Penelope.

"Most everyone is."

"Why does he live alone?"

"Cause he was just a bit free with his fish hooks."

"Fish hooks?"

"Yes, went fishing on land one night by mistake, thought he was pinching a man's shirt off the line, instead of that caught his hook in a pig's ear: awful row. He got away, but they knew who it was. He's always at it. Now he lives up there and no one bothers. Say, what does he do all day?"

"Don't know, makes copra, I think, and gets pearls."

"By golly, he does; best diver in Tuamotus, kill himself one day yet—goes too deep."

"We pinched his canoe and bolted," said Patrick.

"Was he annoyed?"

"Don't know, he was drunk."

"Horribly drunk," said Penelope.

"That fellow not got teaspoon of brains in his skull," said Tommy. "Every time he wants a pearl he just walks about in the lagoon and picks one up. All he does then is buy rum at the Chinaman's. One time I see him come down to Papeete with two big pearls. He sold one, bought a motor car, sold another, bought a house. Two weeks' time no money, so he sells motor car, two more weeks' time he sells house; another week's time he ships back to Tuamotus. And all he take with him is three cases of rum."

"How can we get to Hikueru?" asked Penelope.

"Don't know! Ask Sharkie. Why d'you want to get there?"

"Uncle John is there with a broken leg."

"He's all right, old Doc Murphy is up there. He'll fix his leg if he don't forget which leg it is. Fine surgeon, old Murph, but absent-minded. Last time he operated in London he left his forceps and a pair of scissors in the man's stomach. Just forgot about 'em, thinking of something else. When the patient got home, wife asked for money one day. 'Haven't got any,' he said. 'Yes, you have,' she said, 'I can hear it rattling.' When they found it was the instruments in his innerds, they raised an awful din. By golly it bust poor old Murph; now he's out here running about the Islands, pulls out a tooth for a pound of copra, cuts you open for a couple of pearls and if he kills you doesn't charge a cent; damn decent, most doctors charge double.

"Look," continued Tommy, "there's old Sharkie composing a poem. Never speak to him when he sits on the gunwale; he's getting ideas then. You watch, he hangs his short leg over the water and thinks of the shark, then he gets poetic. Don't ever speak to him when he's composing."

"Is he as fierce as he looks?" asked Penelope.

"Fierce! No, not fierce, gentle as a lamb, has the heart of a child. Course he's killed a few in his day, but only when he had to."

"In the war, I suppose?"

"No, didn't kill anyone in the war; never fired a shot. He says the Turks very nice fellows, didn't see any reason to kill 'em. When he took a prisoner he used to give him a packet of fags and say, '*Haidi*, Johnny, *haidi*!' That means, you run away home. No, he only kills when he's angry."

"Does he often get angry?" asked Patrick somewhat anxiously.

"Golly no, gentle as a child, harmless as a sparrow—when he isn't composing. Watch him, he's coming along now: bet you he's been writing."

Thump—thump—thump. Sharkie swung himself along and sat on the hatch beside them.

"Listen to this! Listen to this! Didn't I tell you I was a poet?

> *"Why do knots grow in the wood?*
> *It's quite ridiculous such things should*
> *Spoil a plane and blunt a chisel,*
> *Seems to me a bit of a swizzle.*

"There! Isn't that fine? Could Mr. Tennyson have written that? Course he couldn't! Could Lord Milton have written that? Course he couldn't!

"COULD HE?" he roared at Patrick.

"No!" said Patrick quickly, "I'm sure he couldn't."

"One day my poems will be printed: *Storm Jibs and Spinnakers*, by William Shanks—then you'll know who's who. *Who's who*, did I say? Listen—Shanks, William. Poet: born Winkfield Row 1883: educated, where was I educated? Never was, wash that out. Recreation, yachting: that's a good one. Author of *Storm Jibs and Spinnakers*, *Wind in the Topsail*, and other poems."

"Will they knight you?" asked Tommy.

"Knight me? Baro-knight me! Sir William Shanks, Bart. —sounds all right. What the yellow devils is that fellow doing at the wheel? Te-ura!" he shouted, "keep her up, keep her up!"

"Land oh!" shouted someone from the bow, "land to port!"

"Marutea," said Sharkie. "Keep her up!"

199

"Ever been there?" asked Tommy.

"Never! Don't want to. All atolls just same thing, reefs and coconut palms, nothing else at all. Sometimes they have a big pass into the lagoon and big sharks inside; sometimes they have little pass and little sharks inside; otherwise all same thing. Creaking crutches! KEEP HER UP!" he roared. "That man's asleep."

CHAPTER NINETEEN

A DUCK AND A WHALE

NEXT morning they were skirting a line of breakers stretching away on their left till it lost itself in the morning haze.

"Keep your eyes skinned," said Sharkie; "watch for the duck."

"Is this Tekopoto?" asked Patrick.

"No fear, this is Duck Island; don't ask any more questions, keep your eyes skinned, and if you see a bird in the water, shout. Where's Vahine, creeping crickets, where's that girl? VAHINE!"

"*Oui, monsieur!*"

Sharkie talked with her awhile in native.

"She says there's two clumps of trees near the wreck," he announced.

"There's a whole blinking forest in front of us," said Tommy, "enough for a dozen wrecks."

The mainsail was dropped, and under foresail and jib they crept in close to the reef.

"Find the duck, find a fortune!" said Tommy.

All hands were scanning the shore. The breeze was light, and, sheltered by the island, the water showed scarcely a ripple. They crept in closer and closer.

"By golly, he's going to wreck us," said Tommy.

Two of the crew were keeping a look out from the rigging. Vahine was watching intently from the deck, but when anyone spoke to her she shook her head.

"Wrong spot," said Tommy; "it's all trees. She says only two clumps; this blinking island is covered with them."

"There's a gap ahead," said Patrick.

"By Jiminee, there is! By jumping Jiminee, you're right. Where's Vahine? VAHINE!"

"*Oui, monsieur!*"

"*Regarde par là!*"

"*Oui, monsieur.*"

"*Les deux groupes?*"

"*Non, monsieur!*"

"There, I told you—wrong island," said Tommy.

A shout from the mast—"*Te toroa!*"

"It's the duck!"

"Where is it?"

"Can't see it. Yes, I can, other side of the reef."

"We're rich," shouted Tommy. "By golly, I knew it, rich, we're RICH!"

He rushed up to Vahine. "*Le Toroa?*" he asked.

202

She shook her head. "*Non, monsieur, il faut trouver les deux groupes des cocos.*"

"*Mais regarde l'oiseau.*"

"*Oui, monsieur, regardez l'oiseau, il prend la fuite.*"

When Tommy looked again a seagull had risen and was flying away.

"Silly ass, it's got its head on anyway," he said. "Wrong island, said it was wrong island."

"*L'autre coté, peut-être,*" said Vahine.

"The other side, perhaps, she says."

But the reef went on far beyond the palm trees, and they were forced a mile or more to sea before they could round the point. Working their way back on the far side they found that the line of coral was not only broken but in places completely absent, so that it was possible to sail much closer in to shore.

Out of the shelter of the island the wind was breaking the surface of the water, making it more difficult to spot anything. Their speed was very much faster than it had been.

> "*The bird that was too tired*
> *To rise up when they fired,*"

chanted Sharkie.

> "*The bird that wasn't dead,*
> *And swam without a ——*"

"ROCKS AHEAD!" shouted the look-out in the bow.

The helm was jammed over, and the schooner came up into the wind.

Down came the foresail with a run, barely missing Tommy, who was standing by the mast. Sharkie was bellowing orders. All round them was a swirl of water, eddying among the out-cropping coral.

"Down jib! Start engine!" Sharkie took the wheel.

"Clams and catfish! That was a near go," said Sharkie, as they threaded their way to safety.

"Fried sole and a haddock, you nearly killed *me*," said Tommy.

A couple of hours later they had lowered the boat and were heading towards two clumps of palms, which Vahine asserted was the direction of the wreck. Patrick was in the bow; Tommy and Tori, one of the crew, were rowing. Penelope, Vahine and Sharkie sat in the stern. Everybody was either watching the surface for some sign of the bird on the masthead, or else peering into the water in search of the wreck itself.

"Wrong island," said Tommy; "too many palms."

"We'll soon know when we get ashore," said Sharkie; "there'll be corpses washed up."

"Crabs would have eaten them," said Tommy.

"There'll be spars off the ship or some sign of humanity."

The flat-bottomed boat rose and fell with the swell. All eyes were turned towards the island, trying to see some trace of wreckage.

"If we could only just drop on that old bird!" The words were hardly out of Tommy's mouth when *scrunch, cranch, scrunch*: a hole was torn in the bottom of the boat.

Tommy was tipped from his seat into Sharkie's arms. Tori fell backwards on top of Patrick. The mast of the *Toroa* had come clean through the bottom and water was flooding in. With every heave of a wave the hole became larger, and there was the old, headless bird beside them in the boat!

"I'll be drowned after all," said Tommy.

204

"Get out and swim," ordered Sharkie, heaving himself over the stern.

"Can't," said Tommy, "never could, born like it."

Everybody else was in the water making for the shore. Tommy, clinging to the duck, was sitting miserably in the boat, now full to the gunwale.

"She can't sink farther; sit where you are, we'll fetch you later," said Sharkie.

"Are there many sharks about?" called Tommy.

"They wouldn't touch you, they hate gin."

"Anyone can have my pearls if they come back quickly," cried Tommy.

The others had nearly reached the shore when a shriek of terror was heard from the little man in the boat.

"SHARK!" he cried, "Shark! No, it's a WHALE! He's coming! Swim! Swim! He's coming."

Those in the water needed no encouragement to swim faster. They could hear confused shouts, but their one idea was to reach the shore.

A horrible peal of laughter came to them across the water: that would be Tommy's last hysterical cry, they thought.

Then silence.

They could hear splashing: that would be his death throes.

Penelope reached the shore. Vahine was there already, sitting in the sand with a queer smile on her face. Patrick and Sharkie had only a few more yards to go. There was no sign of Tori.

Penelope did not dare to look back. There was bound to be blood in the water, perhaps parts of Tommy's mangled body. But why was Vahine smiling?

She let her eyes wander to the scene of the tragedy. Tommy was not in the water, not on the mast; instead, he was sitting in another boat which Tori was busy bailing.

Sharkie rubbed his eyes. "*Are you there*?" he shouted, thinking it was some form of apparition which he saw before him.

"Coming ashore!" called Tommy, as Tori took the oars and rowed towards them.

The boat in which they arrived was covered in green slime, and small shells hung on the timbers.

"Where'd you get her?" asked Sharkie, in amazement. "Tori!"

"She only hold down by two dam' ropes," said Tori; "one cut each rope, she float up quick."

"Off the *Toroa*," said Tommy; "Tori dived."

"He think him shark," said Tori, grinning.

"By golly, you not laugh if you'd seen green bottom come up alongside, just like back of whale. Then old Tori came up other side and blow. Jiminee! Made me jump, he did."

"Did *you* say your prayers?" asked Sharkie.

"You bet I did. I said, please God, no time say much, very sorry all my sins, 'spect I'd do same again. Please God forgive me. Then I look down at whale, ready say good night everybody, think my name Jonah in two tics. What do I see? *Boat*. Upside down. Then Tori turns her over and bails her. I think perhaps one day soon I learn to swim," said Tommy.

"Now we go back and inspect the wreck," said Sharkie.

"And stick on the other mast! I think I stay here and dry my trousers."

Vahine was scrubbing the seats of their new boat with sand and coral. "You come with us," said Sharkie; "time enough dry your trousers when your pockets are full of pearls."

"Gee-rusalem! I forgot them jewels," said Tommy.

The surface of the water was too broken to see more than a vague outline of the hull below them when Tori went down to investigate.

"Wish I could dive," said Tommy.

207

"Wish you could swim," said Sharkie.

"Can you see Tori?"

"Can't see anything. Plague and famine! Don't lurch!"

"How many pearls will he get?" asked Patrick.

"Hundreds," said Sharkie.

"Thousands," said Tommy.

Tori shot head and shoulders out of the water, took a deep breath, and climbed on to the gunwale.

His hands were empty, there was nothing in his feet; perhaps he had them in his mouth or in his *pareu*?

"Got many?" asked Sharkie.

Tori shook his head. "Cabin locked," he said.

"Bust it in," said Tommy, "bust it in."

"You come help too?" asked Tori, with a grin.

"Want a crowbar," said Sharkie.

Vahine exchanged a few words with Tori. "*Il faut chercher la clef,*" she said, and then, cotton frock and all, she slipped into the water.

"By golly she's right—the key. Bet she knows where it is."

Again all heads were over the side trying to glimpse her movements below.

"Swims like an eel," said Sharkie.

"She find nothing," said Tori; "bet captain have key in pocket."

"Can't you bust in a port hole?" asked Patrick.

"Put arm through broken glass, not me! One small cut and sharks here quick."

"Smell blood a mile away," said Tommy.

"Ten miles away," said Tori.

"There's Vahine!"

A shower of spray splashed in their faces as she shook the water from her hair.

"*Pas là!*" she gasped.

"Not there," said Tommy; "we're dished."

"I go down again," said Tori.

"*Il faut du poudre à canon*," said Vahine.

"Gunpowder! She means dynamite. She's right! Got any on board?" asked Tommy.

"What do you take us for, a battle cruiser?" said Sharkie.

"Haven't you got a revolver?"

"What, blow the bolt, with my old Colt?"

"Jiminee Jeroosalem, you got it? Yes! We're *rich*!" shouted Tommy.

"Where's Tori?"

"Still below."

"No, he's not. Here he comes. Any luck, Tori?"

"Pouf—one tin beef," said Tori.

"Can't you bust the door?" asked Tommy.

"Yes! I bust it mighty quick when you give me one small thing."

"What's that?"

"Just one small submarine come whizz bang, then I think door open—p'raps!"

"What about a gun?"

209

"Gun!"

"Yes, you fire shots in lock, then you smash in."

"What about shot in water? S'pose he jump back hit me?"

"We'll give you an extra pearl."

"Wha' for! Wear round neck in heaven? I tell you one thing," said Tori, "that ship down there keep movin'; every time boat on mast rises with wave, ship down below shake herself."

"Can't we lift boat off?"

"I think you best leave where she is. You get heaving on mast, p'raps *Toroa* slip in the deep water again."

"Let's get that gun," said Sharkie.

"Let's get some food," said Tommy.

That evening the schooner lay at anchor, operations having been postponed till the following day. Sharkie had opened a bottle to celebrate the occasion, and was now in poetic mood.

"Do you know," he said, "there's people today calls themselves poets and they can't make two lines rhyme. Blank verse they calls it. Blankety blank verse I calls it! Never mind, if we get those pearls—"

"We've got 'em," said Tommy.

"You shut up and don't interrupt! If you got enough, you go along home and we take the rest. As I was saying, when we get these pearls I'm going to publish my poems."

"Pearls and poems," said Tommy.

"Pearls of poems," corrected Sharkie; "but I'm modest, like all great men; it's only the little ones whose hats get too tight. Eh, Tommy?"

Tommy paid no attention to that remark.

"Where will you publish them?" asked Penelope.

"Listen here, there's only one place to publish poetry—
real poetry, I mean, and that's London. And when I sell
one pearl for £100 I take first class ship to London, then
I sell another pearl and stay at the Ritz, then I publish
my poems. Bound! How do you think they're bound, bet
you'll never guess."

"Banana leaves," said Tommy.

"Sail cloth," said Patrick.

"Native tapa cloth," suggested Penelope.

"Wrong, all wrong. My poems bound in leather, real
leather; what kind of leather do you think?"

"Donkey hide," said Tommy.

"Shut up! Any more guesses? No. I'll tell you—shark
skins, nothing less. Finest leather in the world, grand for
shoes, belts, bags, anything. I've a case of the skins in
Papeete. Got them up in Torres Straits. Went there for
pearls, came back with a load of skins. Yes! The poems of
William Shanks; bound in shark skin, price one quid;
wot they calls a fine edition."

"Got a spare pair of pants?" asked Tommy, getting up.
"Mine are still wet."

"There's a *pareu* in the cabin. You know," he said to the
children, as Tommy went to change, "that man has no soul
for music. I read him poems and I don't believe he listens.
Other night 'fore we met you I wrote one of my best; I'll
read it to you. It's called *Nature*, and there's quite a lot of it.
It begins with very simple things like vegetables, and then
it works up by way of birds to humans, and then it goes
aloft to higher things, and then it whacks down again to
a slug just to show we're all much of a muchness, same as
a keel and a topmast. What's the good of a mast without
a keel, I ask you? Lie flat over and drown itself. What's

211

the good of a keel without a mast? Stick in the mud and grow barnacles.

"Now you listen.

> *What makes a cabbage crinkle?*
> *What makes Brussels sprouts sprout?*
> *What makes a melon swell an'*
> *What makes a pigeon pout?*
> *What makes you live or die?*
> *What gives you styes in the eye?*
> *What makes blood corpuscles*
> *Fight germs inside your muscles?"*

"Can't find that *pareu*," interrupted Tommy, appearing in his shirt.

"There you are!" said Sharkie, "he can't help interrupting. There's only one sound keeps him quiet, it's tweetch—tweetch—tweetch, POP, twickle, twickle, twickle, say when! When he hears that, his soul grows pink and his ears grow red and he pretends he didn't hear—till the glass is full!"

"Where's that blinking *pareu*?" asked Tommy.

"In my cabin, on top of Macbeth!"

"What's that?"

"Blimey! Haven't you heard o' Shakespeare?" said Sharkie. "Wrote poems, same as me."

CHAPTER TWENTY

TOMMY GETS A THIRST, TORI GETS A CHILL

NEXT day the sea was as flat as a mirror; the swell had subsided, and in the seven or eight fathoms where they were anchored they could see the bottom as clearly as most people see across a room.

"Hurry up with that coffee," roared Sharkie. "Son of a sea-louse! What are we here for—a pleasure cruise?"

Black coffee and biscuits were set on the deck.

"Swill it down! Swill it down! Come on, you dawdling dogfish, you languid lump-suckers, over the side and up the pearls. PEARLS! PEARLS! PEARLS!"

"Got the gun?" asked Tommy.

"Got everything. Into the boat, keep her afloat; heave on the oar, aft and fore!" sang Sharkie.

"S'pose gun not fire under water?" said Tori.

"Course it fire under water, you drop down quick, fire six shots in lock; then come up. Next time you go down, door wide open waiting."

"That sound nice," said Tori, "just like cinema picture. I think great pity Tommy not come down too!"

"By golly, I think I learn swim one day soon," said Tommy.

"You watch for *Toroa*," said Sharkie. "Anyone see the old boat? *Can't anyone* see the boat on the mast?"

"See something mighty like it on shore," said Tori.

"She can't have got off the mast," said Patrick.

"She *has* got off! I see her by the pandanus trees. Creeping crayfish! *Where's* the *Toroa*?"

"'Spect she's sunk," said Tori.

"No, she's not, I see her. Keep little bit starboard. Whoa! Way enough. There she is, just the same as yesterday, p'raps little bit on one side."

"How did she move?" asked Patrick.

"Swell," said Tori. "I tell you yesterday the swell keep shake boat on mast."

"Come on," said Sharkie, "load the gun and let him go down."

They had brought a grapnel by which they anchored themselves to the wreck. Tori went overboard with the revolver. The water was as clear as daylight and they could see him catch the shrouds and swing himself on to the deck of the submerged schooner. A moment later he disappeared into the hatchway.

"Hope that gun fires," said Sharkie.

"Hope it fires straight," said Tommy.

"Listen!" said Sharkie.

Everyone kept very quiet, listening for some sort of a bang.

"Can't hear anything," said Patrick.

"Not a sound," said Penelope.

"There's Tori! Here he comes," shouted Tommy.

Tori came to the surface and hung on to the boat for a moment. Then he burst out laughing. "Gun no good," he said, laying it on the seat.

"What! Won't it fire?"

"No need fire—door open all time!"

"The door *open*?" they asked in surprise.

"Yes, door wide open," said Tori; "ship all skew-wiff. Now she fixed on coral she not move."

"Got any pearls?"

Tori shook his head. "I think we look some long while 'fore we find pearls: captain he not dam' fool leave pearls lying all over place."

"Someone been here in the night," said Tommy.

"What y'mean?"

"Ship moved, door open, pearls gone."

"I reckon he hide them alongside his false teeth," said Tori; "somewhere no one likely go look."

Vahine now took her turn at diving.

"Bet they're behind a panel," said Sharkie; "next time you go down look for a splice in the bulkheads."

"Next time I go down I fetch up everything in cabin; time after that I bring up whole ship," said Tori, somewhat sarcastically.

"What about secret drawers in table? Press a spring, out they pop. What about hollow legs in table? Try the frame of the bunk; tap everything. When you find something hollow then we got pearls."

215

"Maybe a false bottom to his sea chest?" said Tommy. "See if you can find any soap—that's a good place to hide things, no one uses it."

"Say, how much wind you think I got?" asked Tori.

Vahine's return was accompanied by a dozen oranges bobbing to the surface.

"*Rien*," she said, "*rien du tout, excepté les oranges qui sont pourries.*"

"Rotten oranges!" said Sharkie, "that's all we find. I tell you, Tommy, right at the start o' this trip; I say to you rotten mangoes, I say to you stinking paw-paws, I say to you we find nothing. I say to you we find no more pearls than hair on my head."

"By golly, I think p'raps you're right, but, by golly, if we find pearls match your eyebrows I think we sit pretty."

Again Tori went down, and again he returned to the surface.

"Yes," he said, "I find cupboard in wall behind bunk. What you think I find there?"

"Rum," said Tommy.

"Oranges!" said Tori. "I think skipper loose in head."

"Not mad; he got boils, can't sit down. Oranges best cure."

"Sacred jellyfish," said Sharkie, "I bring you all the way here to find oranges—*rotten* oranges. Tommy, I think your brain pulp like inside of orange. What you want tell me that story about duck? DUCK! That means nothing! You're right, it's duck we've found, a mighty big egg!"

"If I could swim," said Tommy, "I'd find you hatfuls of pearls."

"If you could swim, you'd 'a been drowned years ago. It's only 'cos you can't swim that everybody saves you."

"Go on, Tori," said Tommy, "try under cabin floor and

when you come up bring lamp with you; p'raps he dropped 'em in the oil bath."

"It's a wash-out," said Sharkie.

"Why not take the spars and ropes?" asked Tommy.

"What for? Want to hang yourself?"

"And spare sails?"

"Sew *you* up in one quick enough, with a lump of lead at your feet."

"Lots of gear on board," said Tommy.

"Did I come here for—" Sharkie's question was cut short by the arrival of more oranges on the surface. Sharkie became inarticulate. A few seconds later Tori appeared.

"Yes," he said, "I find loose plank."

"Where, in floor?"

"Yes, in floor."

"What you find there?"

"Oranges! Cabin full of them, floating up against roof. I think captain make funny joke 'fore he died."

"He had a boil and we've had a stew," said Tommy.

"Can we have a swim?" asked Penelope.

"Yes, you go on an' swim, nothin' else to do. Make it a pleasure cruise! Let's go ashore to the bar, visit the casino. Let's take taxis and drive round the island: everyone drives round the island on a pleasure cruise."

"The farthest side is always the nicest," said Tommy. "If you landed in Eden you'd want to have a look outside. Here, chuck us an orange," he called to Penelope, who was in the water.

"That's bad! Pick us a good one. Rotten shot! Go on—golly, I'm dry—got him! Whoa, that's enough."

"Leave those stinking fruit in the water," roared Sharkie.

"They're not *all* stinking," said Patrick.

"Leave them there anyway. They give me a pain. Oranges! *Oranges*! Pretty pearls, aren't they, Tommy?

> "*Little pearls of gold*
> *Floating in the sea,*
> *Just the thing for Tommy*
> *But they ain't the thing for me.*

Eh, Tommy?"

"Oi did-dee, dee dee," said Tommy. "Look what I've found."

"What?"

"A pearl!"

"Where?"

"In my tooth."

"WHERE?!!!"

"In the orange," said Tommy.

Simultaneously they pounced on two more of the fruit that had been thrown into the boat.

"Another!" shouted Sharkie.

"Three little 'uns," said Tommy. "By golly, we got 'em!"

Meanwhile Vahine and Tori were in the water collecting every bit of yellow they could lay hands on.

"HURROO! HURROO!" shouted Tommy to the children, who were half-way to the shore. "We've GOT 'em! We've GOT 'em!"

"Got what?"

"Pearls! Millions of them. Get those oranges, they're—" but he didn't finish his sentence, for at that moment Sharkie spotted a bit of peel under a floorboard and made a dive for it. Tommy, in his excitement, standing on a seat, lost his balance and went overboard.

"By golly, I find you blinking pearls and then you try

218

to drown me," he said when, after being rescued by Tori, he had recovered his breath.

Nobody paid the smallest attention to his remarks. All four in the water were too busy collecting the floating oranges.

Tori and Vahine took it in turn to dive while Patrick and Penelope retrieved the fruit as it came to the surface.

Half a crateful was already in the boat.

"Bet you all the duds were on top," said Tommy.

"Bet you he never had a boil," said Sharkie.

"Neat, the way he slipped 'em through the peel—one snick of a knife and they're in."

"One snick of my thumb and they're out," said Sharkie, dropping a big one into the bailer.

"Thirty-eight," counted Tommy.

"Thirty-nine! That's a little 'un."

"Forty, forty-one."

"Forty-two, a black boy."

"Forty-three."

"Here's Tori!"

"Any more fruit?"

"No more in cabin," said Tori. "Vahine gone fetch 'em blown on shore. Then all finish." He climbed into the boat, followed by Patrick and Penelope.

"Gee whizz! I think we rich men this time. How many you say you give us?" asked Tori.

"You share third with crew," said Tommy.

"Jews and Gentiles! Never mind shares," said Sharkie. "Dig 'em out! Dig 'em out! Plenty time share later on."

"Fifty-eight."

"Fifty-nine."

"And two, sixty-one."

"I think safer share afore we go back ship," said Tori.

"Those boys tough guys: when they see all we got, p'raps they make trouble."

"When we get back to the ship they'll not see these or see anything else," said Sharkie. "These go in cabin and key go in pocket. Revolver go in pocket too; I don't think we have trouble."

"Five here," said Patrick, "makes sixty-six."

"And three, sixty-nine."

"A big one," said Penelope, "seventy."

"I bet we get £100 for him," said Tommy.

"Put him in the till! Put him in the till!" said Sharkie. "WHAT'S THAT you put in your mouth, Tori?"

"Chew small bit of orange—thirsty!" said Tori.

"You chew one more bit of orange and you chew bit of lead too. See here," said Sharkie, touching the revolver, "you play fair you get fair: you play dirty and you—p'raps you find piece of lead make dirty mark on your skin."

"Eighty-two," said Tommy.

"Eighty-three."

"Eighty-four."

"And two, eighty-six: bet we get the hundred."

"Eighty-eight."

"Eighty-nine."

"Ninety."

"Two stuck together here," said Penelope.

"Put 'em in the bin, sort 'em afterwards."

"Here's a huge one."

"No good; it's blemished."

"Put him in bin."

"Ninety-seven."

"Five little 'uns, hundred and two."

"And two, hundred and four."

"Last round. Come on, cough up a big one."

"Empty!"

"Empty!"

"*Rien!*"

"One small one, hundred and five."

"No more, anyone?"

"No more."

"By golly, hundred and five—ten pounds apiece, a thousand blooming quid!"

"They're not worth that, are they?" asked Patrick.

"I reckon," said Tommy solemnly, "the value of this 'ere lot is one thousand thick 'uns, nowadays called flimsies; once upon a time they was little bits of gold with the King's head, now they're little bits of paper with some bloke's signature."

"I think we go back to ship and get some food, then we come along see if we can't find any more cures for our very bad boils," said Sharkie.

"One thousand pounds. By Jerusalem, that's three hundred for Sharkie, three hundred for me and three hundred clear for Tori and the boys."

"What about us?" said Patrick. "You'd never have found them if I hadn't thrown them at you."

"He's right," said Sharkie.

221

"You never find any at all without me," said Tori.

"You share out with the crew," said Tommy.

"And Vahine?"

"She share out with the crew."

"And captain?"

"He share with himself and finish pay for his blinking ship," said Sharkie.

"And Tommy?"

"By golly, you not find one stale orange peel without me. What you thinking about anyway, not satisfied earn fifty quid in three days?"

"I think you earn three hundred mighty soft," said Tori.

"Blatherumskite, look where you're rowing," said Sharkie. "When we go aboard, those pearls go in safe. After food, we come back find some more, then we talk about divide."

"No more in ship," said Tori.

"Why not?"

"Search everywhere."

"Any bananas below?" asked Tommy. "Or water melons? Have a look for some water melons!"

"Nothin' more in that ship," said Tori. "Store room stove in, everything sunk or rotten."

"We'll have another go this afternoon," said Sharkie.

"By golly, we not half done yet," said Tommy.

The first thing that Sharkie did when he got on board the schooner was to lock the pearls in the big safe built under the cabin bunk. While he was doing this Tommy retrieved his trousers and changed out of his wet *pareu*.

"Here, you keep that key," whispered Sharkie, "you've got pockets; the cabin is mine, the key is yours. Now for some food."

Freshly caught fish, bully beef and half a hank of

bananas were soon demolished, but there had been some delay with Tori's dinner, and while they were waiting for him Tommy dozed in his seat.

"I think I have five minutes' shut eye," said Sharkie, "just five minutes' stretch my one and a half legs in bunk."

The children were eager to be off again and hung about the deck.

Vahine came and joined them.

"Tori got *bellyak*," she said.

"Got what?"

"*Le bellyak—le mal à l'estomac.*"

"Wants a drop of rum," said Tommy; "I'll go find Sharkie."

It turned out to be fever. "My head go round and round this morning, all time in water," said Tori; "one time I think I drown. Now I think I die cold." He was huddled in a corner, shivering, with a bit of sail cloth wrapped round him and his hat pulled over his eyes.

No, he didn't want rum, he didn't want anything, he'd be all right again in the morning.

"'Twould do you good," said Tommy.

No, he didn't want anything, he'd stay where he was; he'd be all right in the morning, then he'd dive again.

"Thought you said there wasn't any more."

"Head bad all morning. Tomorrow I take hand-spike break up cabin, think we find plenty more. Vahine go along today. I come along tomorrow."

"He must be bad not to want rum," said Tommy, when a little later, he and Patrick rowed towards the shore.

"Obstinate as a clam—might as well try to move the reef," said Sharkie.

They were close in to land when Tommy suddenly stopped rowing.

"Mind what you're doing," said Sharkie. "Easy, Patrick. Pull, Tommy! What are you staring at? PULL! or you'll smash us."

"The *Moana*!" said Tommy.

"What's the matter with her?"

"She's moving."

"Rubbish!" said Sharkie.

"She is!" insisted Tommy.

"Swinging with the wind," suggested Patrick.

"Dragging her anchor, perhaps," said Tommy.

"Rot!" replied Sharkie.

"She dragged last night, I'll swear."

"Not an inch!"

"They've got the engine going," said Tommy.

"They WHAT?"

"The sails are going up," said Penelope.

All eyes were on the ship.

"They've skinned us," said Sharkie.

CHAPTER TWENTY-ONE

"NOT TO BE TAKEN"

HALF an hour later Sharkie was sitting solitary and disconsolate on the shore. As Patrick came towards him he was muttering to himself:

> *"Oola moola tahlee*
> *Oola moola tahlee*
> *Kopee aye, kopee aye*
> *Oola moola tahlee.*

"That's what they sing in the Solomon Isles when they're going to eat a man. I'd give Tori *oola moola* if I caught him, string him up over a slow fire and prod him with a spear. Baste him with hot fat too! I'd teach him not to pinch schooners. Fever indeed, the lying shark. Every fish has his own face: I never liked the snout on that skate. No wonder he didn't want any rum; now he's got a case of it. I tell you what, he'll never reach Tahiti, them pearls have a curse on them. They sank the *Toroa* and now they'll sink the *Moana*. I'll bet you my spare leg! No, I can't, they've got that too. What'll I bet you? Haven't got anything! Never mind, they'll never reach Tahiti. They'll be tight as ticks before the night is out and they'll run her on a reef. Sunk they'll be, and sunk we are too, and my poems—GONE!"

"There's plenty crabs on this island if we can catch 'em, and plenty coconuts if we can climb for 'em," said Tommy, joining them, "and on Sundays we'll have a nice salad of young palm tops."

"Go and try the wreck," said Sharkie, sadly. "Take Vahine, maybe she'll find some canned goods."

"Can *we* go?" asked Penelope.

"Yes, you go—rescue Tommy, next time he falls in."

"By golly, I think I stay safe ashore," said Tommy. "Bags I the bottle if you find one," he shouted as Patrick, Penelope and Vahine pushed off in the boat. "You know," he said, turning to Sharkie, "there isn't enough food on this luxurious isle to keep us alive three days."

"Vahine will climb for the nuts, anyway."

"We're splintered," said Tommy.

"We're rammed and sunk," said Sharkie, "we're kiboshed, flyblown, blistered and shanghaied."

"Got any fags?"

"No! Have a cigar?"

"Golly! Where you find those?"

"Bring 'em with me; smoke when I'm rich."

"How many you got?"

"Two. Tori's got the rest along with the pearls. Can't you

see him walking the deck puffing out his cheeks with my cigars, puffing out his pockets with my pearls?"

"Our pearls," corrected Tommy.

"Ours be blowed! They're Tori's now."

"Good cigar," said Tommy, watching the smoke curl away.

"'Course, they're good! Duty free Havana, never opened till today. Lucifer! If I had that swine!"

"Never mind *him*; how are we going to live?"

"We won't, we'll die."

"What about the kids?"

"They'll die too."

"That's rotten, they're too young."

"Doesn't matter when you come to it."

"What d'ye mean?"

"If you're too weak to live, 'tis easier to die—same thing when you too tired stay awake, you falls asleep."

"Not much fun when you're young," said Tommy.

"Not much fun any time, but easy enough when you're ready."

"Vahine will go on living."

"On a berry a day and a raw fish."

"Someone will find her in ten years' time and write a book about it," said Tommy, "*The Island Princess*; *or Queen of the Atoll*, they'll call her. She'll be old and ugly, but they'll say she's young and lovely and they'll dress her up in lots of flowers from the high islands and feed her on fruits that never grew on any atoll, and they'll sell millions of copies of the book and cruise about in a yacht."

"And our bones will be—?"

"Pinched for making fish hooks!"

"These *are* good cigars," said Sharkie.

"Not so sure," said Tommy; "mine makes me a bit queer."

"Queer?"

"Yes, seein' things."

"What you seeing?"

"A ship!" said Tommy.

"Where?"

Sharkie followed the line of his hand. "'Struth! You're right, they're coming back; something's gone wrong."

"Fighting amongst themselves?"

"Drunk!"

"Mutiny!"

"Call the kids."

But the children were already on their way back, for there was nothing worth saving in the wreck. Any stores that might have been there had long since dropped through the hole in her side.

"Found anything?" shouted Tommy, as they neared the shore.

"One bottle," said Patrick.

"Bring it along: that's all we want. Have you seen the ship?"

"Where! Why are they coming back?"

"*Pas le Moana!*" said Vahine.

"Not the *Moana*! Jumping Jimmy she's right, look at her Bermuda mainsail."

"She'll pass us," said Sharkie. "Light a fire! There she goes, on the other tack—I knew it."

"Nip across and wave," said Tommy, making for the other side of the island.

But before he got there, the schooner had gone about again.

"She's heading straight for us," said Patrick.

228

"Where's that bottle?" said Tommy panting. "Golly, I'm dry and blown. Where's that bottle, I say! *Vahine, la bouteille?*"

"*Oui, monsieur!*" said Vahine, producing a small blue bottle.

"Poison!" said Sharkie. "Not to be taken."

"There's no smell," said Tommy, sniffing gingerly. "Looks to me like water," he said, as he poured it on the sand.

"WHAT'S THAT?"

"A pearl!"

Flop. "Another!"

"Go on, shake it."

Flop, flop, flop; three more fell out of the bottle.

"Go on!"

Another, a big one. Flop, flop. "Two more."

"Poison! NOT TO BE TAKEN! Not 'arf! Eight of 'em, big 'uns. Jeemima Jane, and Aunt Maria, never seen better!"

"Where's that blinking ship?"

"Gone about again!"

This time it was Patrick and Penelope who dashed across

the island. The new arrival had dropped her mainsail and was lowering a boat. The rowers pulled ashore and landed.

"What you doing here?" asked a fat red-faced man.

"We've been left," said Patrick.

"Left?"

"Yes! Sharkie and Tommy and me and—"

"Sharkie and Tommy! Where are they?"

"Across the island."

"What are they doing?"

"Looking for pearls."

"Find any?"

"What ho! Jimmy, where'd you come from?" said Tommy, joining the party. "What brought you here—pearls? Golly, I tell you we're trumped. Come on: old Sharkie's over the other side diggin' up the island with his leg. Seen anything of the *Moana*?" he continued. "You have? What, saw her jibe? They're drunk already. Which way was she heading—back to Tahiti? Phew! Here's Sharkie."

"Hullo, Jim!"

"Hullo, Sharks!"

"What you after?"

"Same as you, I guess. Got any?"

"A few."

"Where did you find 'em?"

"Take us on board and I'll tell you."

"We thought of staying here awhile," said Jameson.

"What for? Nothing here!"

"Oh, just a rest, men a bit tired, you know. We're going along to explore the lagoons up around Amanu."

"Come a bit out of your way, didn't you?"

"P'raps little bit; old fool Terii got fed up with the compass jiggling about, drove a wedge in it to keep it still!"

"I've heard that story before, told it myself once or twice. I reckon you're after the *Toroa*."

"You found her?"

"Yep!" said Sharkie.

"Found any pearls?"

"Hundred and five."

"Where are they?"

"On board the *Moana*."

"*Moana*?"

"Sure thing! Can you catch her?"

"Depends on the wind."

"It's rising."

"Come on! Let's hop it."

"Don't be so personal," said Sharkie, as he caught Patrick and Tommy by the scruffs of their necks and bounced across the island.

"Crowd it on," said Sharkie, once they were aboard. "Crowd it on! Haven't you got topsails? Crowd 'em on! Flying jib? Shoot it up! I tell you they're worth thousands."

"Big as eggs," said Tommy, " big as hens' eggs."

"Have a drink," said Jameson.

"Thanks," said Tommy. "Big as ostrich eggs!"

The wind was full astern and increasing every moment.

"She won't carry it," said Jameson.

"Let her rip," said Sharkie. "Hang out your shirts! Hold up your hats! Drive her through it!"

"Wish I'd brought my umbrella!" sighed Tommy.

"The *Moana's* foul," said Sharkie; "half a reef on her bottom, should 'a been scraped. Can't you rig a spinnaker?"

"We'll catch her by morning," said Jameson.

"You wouldn't if I was on board!" said Sharkie. "Where's that food we heard about?"

231

"How long did you reckon to stay on that island?" asked Jameson after he had heard their account of Tori.

"Food for three days," said Tommy.

"Then you'd draw lots, eh?"

"By golly, I think we all go home to our mothers on crutches."

"None of your jokes on my leg," said Sharkie. "Say, what d'you think of this?—

> *"You can't live long*
> *On a coral reef*
> *'Cos you can't eat the tins*
> *When you've finished the beef;*
> *And you can't stop your thirst*
> *When you're sweaty hot*
> *'Cos you can't drink the water*
> *Wot you haven't got!"*

"Too topical," said Tommy.

"English ain't good!" said Jameson. "Say, wind's going round."

"Let her rip," said Sharkie. "I'll have my ship in the morning. That's a good line! What rhymes with morning?"

"Warning," said Penelope.

"Full marks," said Sharkie.

"How are you going aboard when we do catch up?" asked Patrick.

"Ram her," said Tommy.

"Maggots alive! Sink my ship? No blinking fear!" said Sharkie.

"Lose the pearls too," said Jameson.

"Fire a shot," suggested Tommy, "across her bows, like the pirates."

"Got any guns, Jimmy?" asked Sharkie.

"·22 Winchester."

"Any lead?"

"Box o' fifty."

"Ought to hit once, anyway!" said Tommy.

"YOU aren't going to waste shot; you're the landing party!" said Jameson.

"*Me*?" said Tommy.

"Yes! You. You go along under cover of gun, knock out all the crew, bring back the jewels," said Sharkie.

"*Alone*? S'posing I fall in the water?"

"Then you swim!"

"You stay here, Admiral!" said Sharkie. "I take my own ship. What's more, I do the shooting. Six little ·455's in my gun, one for each of them. I reckon they very glad come alongside."

The *Hinano* was lunging through the water; white-capped waves chased her and fell astern, large combers lifted her and pushed her forward. The night was thickening. Every star had vanished. Nothing could be seen but phosphorescent spray.

"It's coming up fresh!" said Jameson.

"Keep her to it," said Sharkie.

Squalls of rain now blew along and compelled them to shelter in the cabin, all but Jameson, who stayed at the wheel. The children dropped off to sleep in the bunks. Sharkie sat at the table scribbling on bits of paper. Tommy snored in his chair.

"Morning—warning," muttered Sharkie, "warning—morning doesn't seem to work. How can I write with that snoring going on?"

"Do leave my feet alone," grumbled Patrick from his bunk.

"There's no one touching you! Ship in the morning, never a warning."

"Someone's tickling my head," said Penelope.

Tommy snored louder than ever.

"No place for a poet!" said Sharkie, getting up in desperation.

He came on deck and balanced himself beside the wheel.

"Going to blow," said Jameson.

"Keep her to it!"

"She'll never carry it."

"Drive her on," said Sharkie.

Suddenly the children were awakened by a report like a gun. The ship swung into the wind. People rushed about on deck.

"Battle's begun," said Tommy, yawning.

The noise and commotion on deck increased. "Regular war on," he said, peering up the hatchway.

"Who's winning?" asked Penelope.

"Can't see, too dark, they're chuckin' all the furniture about."

"The revolver's here," said Patrick.

"By golly, so it is!"

Tommy rushed up on deck brandishing the weapon. Blocks and tackle were flapping in all directions. Sharkie was at the wheel. Jameson and the crew were making fast the tattered foresail.

Tommy searched round for sight of the *Moana*.

"Put that gun down," said Sharkie; "there's enough trouble on board."

"Sunk?" asked Tommy.

"Sunk and splintered," said Sharkie. "Split from head to foot!"

"Who? Tori?" asked Tommy.
"No! The foresail and US!"

Now that there was no hope of catching the *Moana*, the mainsail was reefed and they ran before the ever increasing

wind. The children went back to their bunks. Tommy put his legs on the table and pulled his hat over his eyes. Sharkie scribbled on paper and growled.

"You lose pearls, I lose poems! The work of years. Last night I tie 'em all up in one bundle ready take with me to London. William Shanks, Poet of the Pacific, C/o the Ritz."

"Can't you remember them?" asked Tommy.

"Never could, never could, I write 'em once, then forget 'em. Look at this:

235

> *"Landsmen talk of romance at sea*
> *Hey diddle diddle, ho diddle dee!*
> *They oughter come out in a schooner with me*
> *Hey diddle diddle-dee."*

"That's good," said Tommy encouragingly. "That's *very* good."

> *"They write with joy of the white sea foam*
> *Ho diddle diddle, hey diddle dee!*
> *Sittin' most comfy on their tails at home*
> *Hey diddle diddle—dee."*

"Fine!" said Tommy, "first class."

> *"They think how noble at sea to starve*
> *Hey diddle, ho diddle dee!*
> *While they ask their wife wot there is to carve.*
> *Not arf!—they don't diddle me."*

"Your best," said Tommy; "couldn't be better."

"It *could* be better, I've forgotten half—all about seein' 'em wet to the skin, icicles hanging on their nose and chin, something something sweating in the sun, no iced drinks when day's work done. I tell you 'twas a masterpiece: couldn't 'a been written by any other hand. True Shanks, that was.

"And this one," he continued rather sadly, "this one was fine too.

> *"'Tisn't very funny for a tunny to be tinned*
> *And a sardine soused in oil can see no humour*
> *In the faces of his friends, heads and tails to either ends—*

"And there it's me that's canned—I can't remember the last line."

236

"Sardines haven't got heads," said Tommy.

"A poet has licence," said Sharkie.

"Don't forget you're dedicatin' that book to me," said Tommy. "The pearls isn't lost yet."

Patrick kicked in his sleep.

Penelope twisted and turned and scratched her head.

Tommy pulled his hat farther over his eyes and snored again.

Sharkie went on scribbling.

CHAPTER TWENTY-TWO

"THEY KNOW US THERE!"

WHEN Penelope woke up next morning she was staggered to see thick strands of her own hair lying on the pillow. When she ran her hands over her head she discovered large bare patches of skin.

"Mange," said Patrick, rubbing his eyes, "or scabies. Something dirty you've picked up—ringworm p'raps. Here, don't shake it over me. Gosh, something's happened to my feet."

"You've got it too!" said Penelope.

The soles of his feet were almost raw, and so tender that he could hardly walk on them.

"By golly, they got you!" said Tommy. "Cockroaches, Jiminee yes! Eat you alive."

On deck they were busy fixing a new foresail but by the time it was hoisted the wind had dropped and for all the use it was it might have stayed in the locker.

It was decided that any further attempt to catch the *Moana* was useless. By this time Tori would be well away, and goodness only knew in what direction he had sailed. It certainly would not be to Tahiti, where the schooner was known and where awkward questions would be asked.

With the exception of Tommy, everyone on board was depressed. Jameson swore at the loss of his sail. Sharkie swore at the loss of his ship. They all lamented the fortune that had been so nearly in their grasp.

For two days they laboured along with scarcely wind

enough to fill their sails. Then Jameson decided to run in to Anaa island, on chance of a load of copra.

"Caught it here a few years back," said Sharkie.

"Caught what?" asked Patrick.

"Blooming cyclone, worst ever known, swept everything before it; trees, houses, pigs, chickens, and hundreds of inhabitants. All the schooners sunk: even the bones washed out of the graves."

"Only thing I know about it," said Jameson, "is the caves; place is full of them, down in the coral. You can wander for miles once you get inside. What me? No fear, too deep. Couldn't swim down. Several natives hid there for months after killing a French gendarme."

"Good place for Tori," suggested Patrick.

"You're right. That's a chance!" said Tommy. If the *Moana* is there, that's where he'll be. Who'll go after him?"

"Why *you*, of course!" said Sharkie.

There was no sign of the *Moana* at Anaa, neither was there any copra because all the men had gone to Hikueru for the pearl fishing. There was no reason to stay, and now that the wind was freshening they would make better speed towards Tahiti. So off they sailed once more.

Next day, however, the wind fell light again. In the distance they could see whales spouting.

"Them whales have all the wind," said Tommy. "Watch 'em blow! Over there on the horizon; see 'em—count the spouts!"

"Blow once for every foot of their length," said Jameson, "and every foot weighs one ton; and when they dive, they stay below one minute for every ton."

"His father was a whaler," said Tommy. "Swallowed by a whale, wasn't he, Jimmy?"

239

"Crushed in the ice," said Jameson.

"Start that blinking engine and let's get a move on," said Sharkie.

"He's getting irritable," said Tommy; "long holidays *are* a mistake!"

"Feeds on giant squids, the sperm whale does," said Jameson. "None of the others could swallow a herring."

"Garn!" said Tommy, "I've seen one thrown up on shore and he had a mouth like Trafalgar Square."

"Yes, and a gullet like a hosepipe; he wasn't no sperm."

"His mouth was full of whalebone."

"That's right; sieves out the water when he takes a mouthful of shrimps same as a duck dibbles in the mud."

"Never knowed that before," said Tommy.

"START THAT ENGINE!" roared Sharkie.

With the wind astern it was impossible to get away from the fumes: port or starboard, forrard or aft, it was the same thing, petrol and stale oil.

Eventually Patrick and Penelope, being assured that cockroaches would not attack in daylight, went below to the cabin to sleep.

"Didn't get a blooming wink last night," said Penelope.

"Ship ahead!" said the man at the wheel.

"Dismasted!" said Jameson.

"The *Moana*," said Sharkie, "we've got her—masts blown out."

"*Mitiaro*," said the helmsman.

"The what?"

"It's the *Mitiaro*!"

"By golly, he's right, the launch from Tahiti."

"Heading for us, too," said Jameson.

"Seen anything of the *Moana*?" shouted a white man as the launch came alongside them a few minutes later.

240

"Wish we could!" yelled Sharkie.

"Hullo, Uncle," called Tommy. "You looking for the kids?"

"Have you seen them?" replied Uncle John, for indeed it was he who had hailed them.

"Come on board and I'll tell you," called Tommy.

Next day the schooner was back in Tahiti, and a fortnight later Tommy and Sharkie were on the pier to see Uncle John and the two children leave in the mail boat.

"Don't open this till you're at sea," said Tommy, pressing a small package into Patrick's hands.

Then the hooter sounded, the gangway was raised, ropes were cast off and the clear water of the lagoon was churned into foam. "See you soon in England," called Tommy, as the ship started on her ten-day voyage to Sydney.

When they were outside the reef and had gone down to inspect their cabins, Patrick opened his parcel. In a match box, wrapped in cotton wool, were two fine pearls. "One for Penelope, one for Patrick; wages from the *Moana*."

"I thought they were all stolen, except the big ones from the bottle," said Alexander.

"Must have had them at home," said Penelope.

"Wonder what they're worth?" said Patrick.

One day in New Zealand, ten days in Sydney, then on board an Orient liner for home. Melbourne, Adelaide, Fremantle, across the Indian Ocean to Colombo. Port Said *via* the Red Sea and Suez Canal, and then a week in the Mediterranean, calling at Naples, Toulon and Gibraltar.

How cold and grey the low shores of England looked as they approached, but how good to be back again!

"Wisha God be praised!" said Mary Kate, "and they never took a bite out of ye at all."

It was two months since they had left Tahiti, and now they were walking up Bond Street with the contents of Tommy's match box in Uncle John's pocket.

They stopped outside a window, imposing in the simplicity of its decorations. Nothing but black velvet, and in the centre one double necklace of pearls.

"This seems our mark," said Uncle John, "Leave it all to me and don't look surprised at anything."

"Posh," whispered Patrick, as they passed through the revolving doors.

After they had explained the purpose of their visit, the assistant showed them into the manager's office. He was a little bald man with sharp beady eyes hidden behind tortoise-shell glasses.

"Not very good colour," he said, looking at the pearls, "not very good colour." The shape was good, but they would have to skin them, he said. That would of course reduce their size, but it might improve their lustre. They were very overstocked just then and people were not buying. Of course, if they had been a pair, or if they had happened to fit a special necklace, then he could have made a better offer, but as it was, just to put them into stock—well, he could not offer more than—um—well, he didn't really want them but he would give—um—£150 for the two.

"I reckoned on double that," said Alexander.

"Oh, but no—not today. Two years ago, yes, but not today." No. He was sorry.

"Never mind," said Alexander carelessly, and made as if to take the pearls.

But the little man interrupted him. "Excuse me one moment," he said, "I will ask my partner; perhaps he may have some special use for them."

He rang the telephone.

"My partner, he does all the matching, he is a great artist, a very great artist."

The door opened and the great artist came in; that is to say, a large expanse of waistcoat first appeared, followed by a black coat on top of which was a face the colour of a pillar box.

He seemed deaf and dumb, and the little man in glasses carried on a rapid conversation with him in gestures. Then they both examined the pearls again, weighed them and gesticulated to each other.

"He thinks we can give you two hundred, if you will accept that," said the manager.

"Guineas?" asked Alexander.

The artist nodded.

The manager took out his cheque book. Pay to John Alexander Esq. the sum of two hundred and ten pounds sterling.

"Yes! I thank you, they are nice pearls. My partner he says he can use them for a pair of ear-rings. Yes, that is why I can pay you the higher price. I am glad I asked him."

"So am I!" muttered Alexander, as the door closed

243

behind him. "Didn't expect to get half that," he said as they got back into the street.

"Now for lunch! Where shall we go?"

"We're rich," said Patrick; "the Café Royal."

They sat down in Alexander's favourite corner of the restaurant, on the left of the entrance.

"Two gentlemen been looking for you all the week, sir!" said George, the waiter.

The chief superintendent came along and shook hands. "Glad to see you back. Two friends of yours looking for you every day. No, I don't know their names: one a little lame, not much hair, says he met you in Tahiti."

At that moment a small face appeared round the glass screen.

"Tommy!" said Patrick.

"By golly, it's them!" said Tommy, rushing in.

"IT'S THEM!" roared Sharkie, waving his arms.

George dodged the human windmill and pulled up another table.

"How did you get here?" asked Alexander.

"Across America. Left a month after you did. Got here last week."

"What brought you over?"

"Pearls," said Sharkie.

"Pearls?" asked Alexander, a bit surprised.

"Yes, the *Moana*."

"But, did you find her?"

"No, she sank," said Tommy. "Go on, Sharks, you tell them."

"Clams and codfish! Tommy pinched the pearls out of the safe and carried them in his belt all the time."

"By golly! I didn't trust Tori and his *bellyak*," said Tommy.

"Why didn't you tell us?" asked Penelope.

"No fear, one chance is enough."

"Didn't Tori get any?"

"Not one, by Jiminee!"

"Made much?" asked Alexander.

"Thousands!" said Tommy, "and more to sell."

"Where are you staying?"

"At the Ritz," said Sharkie. "Ask for William Shanks, Poet of the Pacific. They know us there."

LAGOON
HUT
THREE PALM
PAHEERO'S
ISLAND
FIRST LANDING
REEF PASS
OCEAN